Jonatha

Terrance Dicks lives in Hampstead in a big old house with one wife, three sons, two cats and a large hairy dog. He has been a writer for longer than he cares to think about and has written more books than he can count including seventy odd *Doctor Who* books. He has written the following for Piccadilly Press:

THE GOOD, THE BAD AND THE GHASTLY: WORLD WAR TWO
THE GOOD, THE BAD AND THE GHASTLY: THE WILD WEST
THE UNEXPLAINED: THE WOLLAGONG INCIDENT
THE UNEXPLAINED: THE BERMUDA TRIANGLE INCIDENT
HARVEY TO THE RESCUE
HARVEY ON HOLIDAY
HARVEY AND THE BEAST OF BODMIN
HARVEY GOES TO SCHOOL

Text copyright © Terrance Dicks, 1989 (Spitfire Summer),
1989 (The School Spirit), 1991 (Jonathan and the Superstar)

Illustration copyright © Adriano Gon,
1989 (Spitfire Summer),
1989 (The School Spirit), 1991 (Jonathan and the Superstar)

This volume copyright, 1997

Printed and bound in India by Thomson Press for the publishers Piccadilly Press Ltd.,
5 Castle Road, London NW1 8PR

A catalogue record for this book is available from the British Library

ISBN: 1 85340 428 4 (hardback)
1 85340 462 4 (trade paperback)

Jonathan's Ghost

Terrance Dicks
Illustrated by Adriano Gon

Piccadilly Press • London

Contents

Spitfire Summer

CHAPTER ONE

Dogfight

The two fighter planes wheeled and whirled and swooped about one another in the bright blue summer sky.

One bore red, white and blue circles on the wings, the other the crooked black cross of the Nazi Swastika. British and German, Spitfire and Messerschmidt . . .

Suddenly the British plane seemed to gain the advantage. Swooping dangerously close to its opponent, the Spitfire looped first under then high above it, then swooped down out of the sun, machine-guns blazing. Smoke pouring from its fuselage, the Messerschmidt went into a spin, spiralling down towards the ground.

But the Spitfire had not escaped un-harmed. A thin spiral of smoke was coming from one wing and the engine had an erratic staccato note. Slowly the wounded Spitfire limped across the sky, struggling desperately to recover the safety of its home base . . .

Jonathan awoke sweating, his heart pounding furiously. For a moment he stared dazedly at the blue sky outside his bedroom window, as if somehow he was still out there with the duelling planes. He sat up on one elbow, rubbing his eyes, coming slowly back into the real world, realising it had only been a dream.

His alarm went off with a clatter and he reached out and switched it off.

His mother's voice came floating up the stairs. "Are you awake, Jonathan? You don't want to miss your train."

Jonathan grinned. Good old Mum, he thought. Instant hassle the minute you got your eyes open. "On my way, Mum," he yelled and jumped out of bed.

After a hasty wash at the handbasin in the corner of his room, Jonathan scrambled into his clothes. His rucksack, already packed,

was in the corner by the door. Shoving his
toilet things into their waterproof bag,
Jonathan jammed it into the rucksack and
did up the straps. "Jonathan!" came his
mother's voice again.

"Coming, Mum," yelled Jonathan. But
instead of leaving he paused and looked
round the room. "Well, this is it," he said
cheerfully, addressing the empty air. "Soon
as I've had my toast, Mum'll drive me to the
station."

There was no reply. The empty room stayed empty. "Be good while I'm away," he said. "No getting up to mischief and scaring the neighbours."

Still nothing. "Oh, come on Dave, stop sulking," said Jonathan. "I know it's a bit rough on you my going away by myself, but there's weeks of the summer holidays to go yet and I'm going crazy stuck here at home. Great-Aunt Caroline's invitation was a life-saver. She even sent me the train ticket . . . "

Still there was no reply.

Jonathan shrugged. "All right, then, suit yourself. If you don't want to say goodbye, then don't. See you in a fortnight."

As Jonathan picked up his rucksack and turned towards the door he caught a flicker of movement in the corner of his eye. He turned and saw a shape appear, materialising on the end of his bed.

It was the form of a boy of about his own age, wearing shorts, grey socks wrinkled down around the ankles, grimy white tennis shoes and an open-necked cricket shirt. The boy's hair was cropped in a forties short-back-and-sides, his normally cheerful face was set

in an evil scowl. His name was Dave, and he was Jonathan's best friend. He was also a ghost, killed when a bomb hit this very same house in the war.

"Ah, so there you are," said Jonathan cheerfully. "I knew you wouldn't let me go without saying goodbye."

Dave still didn't speak. Instead, he twisted his face into an even more hideous scowl, stuck out his tongue, then put the thumb of his outstretched hand to his nose and wawggled the fingers in the traditional gesture of insult. Still in this same position, he faded slowly away.

Jonathan sighed, and carried his rucksack downstairs. Sometimes it wasn't easy being friends with a ghost.

Over the toast and marmalade, his mother sounded both puzzled and pleased at the same time. "It's very nice of your Great-Aunt Caroline to ask you to stay with her, but it's a bit strange as well."

"Strange how?" asked Jonathan through a mouthful of toast. "She must have heard how amazingly lovable I am."

His mother gave him a doubting look. "Well, maybe. The thing is, she's never wanted to have very much to do with the rest of the family before this."

"Maybe she's thinking of making me the heir to the family fortune," said Jonathan hopefully.

"That's just it, there isn't one. She lives in this big old house in the country all by herself. She's too poor to keep it up properly and too obstinate to sell it."

"Any other relatives about?"

"I don't think so. There was a nephew, a bit of a bad lot, but he got killed in the war I think, or maybe just disappeared. There was

6

something odd about it all. Some kind of family scandal that got hushed up." Jonathan's mother gave him a worried look. "If she is thinking about making you her heir, mind you don't go doing anything to spoil it. And watch your manners, Great-Aunt Caroline's one of the old school."

Jonathan looked at his watch. "Well, she won't be very impressed if I miss my train then, will she? We'd better get a move on."

*   *   *

Jonathan's mother had a busy day ahead of her, so she just dropped him off at the station, telling him at least three times not to get on the wrong train. Jonathan found the right train without too much trouble.

Choosing an empty carriage, he put his rucksack in the luggage rack, installed himself in a corner seat facing the engine and sat back, enjoying the luxury of his surroundings.

He wasn't left in peace for very long.

Two prosperous-looking, plump, red-faced young men, loaded down with umbrellas,

suitcases, briefcases and copies of all the more serious-looking newspapers, burst into the compartment and sat down, spreading themselves and their possessions over most of the seats, and talking all the time in loud voices. "So I said to J.B.," one of them bellowed, "J.B., I said, fifty million is definitely the bottom line. Well, he saw right away I meant business and climbed down at once . . . "

Jonathan gave a sort of internal groan and decided to go and look for somewhere quieter.

He was just about to stand up and get his rucksack when he realised that the older of the two men was glaring at him disapprovingly.

8

"I say, little boy, you're in First Class. Off you go now!"

Jonathan sat tight. He wouldn't have moved now for the world. He just sat and stared out of the window.

The train gave a sudden jolt and began drawing slowly out of the station.

The man leaned forward. "Did you hear me, boy? This is a First Class compartment."

Jonathan turned to look at him. "I'm perfectly well aware of that, thank you," he said politely.

"Now look here, I don't want any cheek. This is a First Class compartment and you need a First Class ticket to travel in it."

"Yes, I know that too, thank you."

By now the man was losing patience. "Have you got a First Class ticket?" he shouted.

Now Jonathan wasn't normally rude to strange adults, or to anyone else for that matter. Generally speaking he was a good-natured and fairly polite sort of boy. But if there was one thing that really made him mad it was the sort of grown-up who felt politeness was a one way street, that they

9

could be as rude as they liked, but still expected kids to treat them with respect. Now the second man joined in. He spoke slowly, loudly and very distinctly, the way some people speak to children or foreigners. "Do you have a First Class ticket?"

Jonathan leaned forward and spoke with equal clarity. "Are you a ticket collector, then? Because if you're not, I really don't see that it's any of your business."

The man began spluttering with rage. "Cheeky little oik. I've a good mind to throw you out myself."

He lunged forward, reaching for Jonathan's collar.

But somehow things went wrong.

His feet seemed to slide from under him, and he landed on the floor of the compartment.

His friend reached out to help him, but somehow he tripped up too, falling heavily on top of the man he was trying to help.

The two men thrashed about wildly, trying to extricate themselves from the narrow space and get up. Somehow the more they struggled the worse things became.

Their briefcases burst open, filling the air with important-looking papers. In his struggle to get free, one of the men caught his friend a painful clip over the ear, and moments later the second man's elbow connected with the end of his attacker's nose.

"Tickets please," said a new voice as the compartment door slid open. A tall, stern-faced ticket collector stood in the doorway, looking down in amazement at the two dusty, struggling figures on the floor. "Now then, what's going on here?"

"No idea," said Jonathan cheerfully. "These two came in shouting and then they seemed to get into a fight. I reckon they're drunk if you ask me."

The ticket collector helped the two men to disentangle themselves and get to their feet. They dusted themselves down, stuffing their papers back in their briefcases. Once they were more or less sorted out the older man said, "It's all this kid's fault. He's got no right to be in this compartment and he refused to show us his ticket."

"No reason why he should, sir," said the collector calmly. "That's my business not yours." He turned to Jonathan and said solemnly, "Tickets please!"

Equally solemnly, Jonathan produced his ticket and handed it over.

The ticket collector studied it, clipped it and handed it back. "All in order sir, thank you." Luckily Jonathan's unknown Great-Aunt Caroline had paid for him to travel in style.

He turned to the two men who had been watching all this in amazement.

"Tickets please."

Sulkily the two men began reaching for their wallets.

The wallets weren't there.

Frantically the two men searched all their pockets but with no success. The ticket collector was stony-faced. "If you don't have any tickets, gentlemen, I shall have to ask you to purchase them."

"How can we?" screamed the older man. "Our money's in our wallets with the tickets. Don't be such a fool."

"No need to be abusive, sir," said the collector stolidly. "I think you'd better come with me and see the Chief Guard."

"I bet that kid's got something to do with it," the older man began.

The younger man said, "Don't make matters worse, Freddy. We were only in here a few minutes and the kid didn't come any-where near us. We must have had our pockets picked in that crowd, when we went through the barrier."

Protesting furiously, the older man let himself be led away.

When the compartment was empty again, Jonathan sat back and looked around.

"All right, Dave, I know you're around. Come out, wherever you are."

For a moment nothing happened. Then a voice came from above his head. "Wotcher, mate!"

Jonathan looked up. Hands behind his head, Dave lay stretched out on the luggage rack, using it like a hammock.

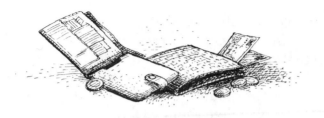

CHAPTER TWO

Haunted

"How did you know I was here?" asked Dave.

Jonathan sighed. "With all that chaos and confusion going on? Of course I knew you were here. Come on, hand 'em over!"

For a moment Dave looked blank. Then, "Oh, you mean these?" Two expensive looking wallets appeared in his hands. He chuckled. "Wonder what they'll do now? Maybe they'll have to work their passage, stoke the engine or something."

"Diesels don't need stoking," said Jonathan. "You'd better give those wallets back."

"What, and spoil all the fun?"

"You've already had your fun. I'm all in favour of teaching those twerps a lesson, but stealing's going too far. Anyway, one of them's already tried to accuse me. If those wallets are found here I'll be in real trouble. Go on, you give them back."

"All right, then, hang on," said Dave and vanished.

Jonathan sat staring at the outskirts of London as they flashed by the window. He had rather mixed feelings about Dave turning up. Dave's well-meant attempts at being helpful had caused Jonathan no end of trouble at school, and it looked as if very much the same thing might happen on this holiday.

Suddenly Dave reappeared, this time sitting on the seat beside him. "All taken care of. I put the wallets in their briefcases. They'll think they fell out in the struggle and got shoved in the cases by mistake. They're bound to find them sooner or later."

"Where are they now?"

"In the guard's van, having a hell of a row with the guard." Dave chuckled. "He still insisted they'd got to pay their fare, so they searched all their pockets and came up with a few crumpled notes and some change. In the end they managed to scrape up two fares between them. But this is the good bit. They didn't have enough for First Class, so they're going to have to go Second."

Jonathan burst out laughing. "Serve them right, they can see how the other half lives. Well, that takes care of them, now what about you?"

"How do you mean?"

"Well, what are you doing here?"

Dave looked hurt. "Aren't you glad to see me?"

"I suppose so," said Jonathan, and to be honest he was quite pleased. "But I thought you were tied to haunting the house? I mean, you can't haunt a train, can you?"

"Only if it's a ghost train," said Dave. He laughed at his own awful joke, then became serious again. "It's not only places that get haunted, it's people as well." He looked solemnly at Jonathan. "I, me old mate, am now haunting you. So, where you go, I go. Isn't that terrific?"

Jonathan sighed. "Terrific." He remembered, long ago, reading a ghost story called 'The Haunted Man.' Now, here he was, a haunted boy. It didn't have quite the same ring to it, but he supposed the principle was the same.

"Right then," said Dave cheerfully. "Now, where are we off to, and who's this old trout Great-Aunt Caroline?"

"She's my mother's aunt," said Jonathan. "From the posh side of the family, or at least, from the once-posh. Now she lives all alone in a big old house in Kent, right on the coast. So, at least we're going to the seaside."

"What, like Southend?" said Dave happily. "Cockles and whelks and candy-floss, rides on the scenic railway and boat trips round the harbour. Any more for the Skylark?"

"What?"

"That's what the boat man used to say. His boat was called the Skylark. When you were out at sea he stopped rowing and collected the fares. Anyone who couldn't pay had to swim back."

"I don't think this place is exactly Southend," said Jonathan. "I looked it up on the map. It's a tiny little place right out on the sea end of the Thames Estuary, miles from anywhere by the looks of it."

Dave sniffed. "Probably nothing there but sea and mud-flats."

"Apparently there used to be a big airfield there during the war," said Jonathan, trying to make the place sound a bit more interesting. "Spitfires used to fly out of it during the Battle of Britain."

Jonathan had a sudden quick flash of fighter planes circling in a blue sky, and suddenly he remembered his dream. He couldn't help feeling that the dream was very important, that his journey and the dream were somehow linked . . .

For a moment he sat staring out of the window. Then he shivered, and looked at his watch. "Anyway, we'll know before very long, it's not that long a journey really. We have to change at the end of the line and get some little local train . . . "

Despite Dave's arrival, the rest of the journey passed off without any more excitement. Jonathan ate the sandwiches his mother had insisted on providing, and got himself a coke from the buffet. On the way he caught sight of the two men from his compartment. They were sitting in a crowded Second Class compartment, surrounded by a jolly mum and dad with three lively, noisy children, all off to a day at the seaside. The littlest kid kept tipping one of the men's bowler hats over his eyes and roaring with laughter. The two men didn't look happy, but the kids were having a wonderful time.

*   *   *

Following the instructions in Great-Aunt Caroline's letter, they eventually changed from the big train, parting company with the jolly holiday-bound crowds and got onto a little local diesel.

The odd thing was that the two business-suited, bowler-hatted men changed with them.

They must have found the wallets, because Jonathan spotted them hurriedly buying tickets. However, the train was so small that it didn't even have a First Class carriage, and Jonathan took care to keep well away from them. This little train was nearly empty, so

he was able to sit and chat with Dave.

At the moment, Dave, quite real and solid to Jonathan but invisible to anyone else, was sitting opposite him in the empty carriage staring out of the window. He wasn't much impressed with what he was seeing, just flat green fields fringed by mud-flats and the misty sea in the distance.

"Looks like the end of the world to me.

What on earth are we going to do here?"

Jonathan shrugged. "Go for nice long walks, do a bit of bird watching."

"Terrific!"

"Look, you're not even supposed to be here, so for goodness sake lay low and keep out of mischief. Great-Aunt Caroline must be pretty ancient by now and I don't want you to scare her into popping off."

"Me, get into mischief?" said Dave looking hurt. "As if I would . . . "

They were drawing into a tiny station by now and Jonathan looked out of the window at the sign. "Marsh Halt. Come on, we're here!"

Grabbing his rucksack, Jonathan got off the little train.

Only two other people got off the train with him – the two businessmen he'd had trouble with earlier.

"I wonder what they're up to," said Jonathan. He turned to Dave, only to find that he'd disappeared.

The two men glared indignantly at Jonathan for a moment, then decided to pretend he didn't exist.

Jonathan did the same and they all walked off the platform determinedly not seeing each other.

Outside the little station there was nothing but an empty country lane. Jonathan stood looking round him helplessly. Not far away, the two businessmen were doing exactly the same thing, still pretending that he was invisible.

A little old man with a brown wrinkled face and a bald head with a fringe of white hair emerged from the tiny station and stood blinking at them in amazement. Probably the first time anyone has ever got off here, Jonathan thought.

One of the two men called, "I say, old chap, any chance of a taxi? We want to get to the local inn."

The old chap gave a sort of dry creaking sound which, Jonathan realised, must be a chuckle. "Pub be two moile down the road," he said, pointing. "And there ain't been no taxi here since nineteen fifty-three."

He turned and shuffled back into the station.

Suddenly a sort of rattling, chugging sound

came from the opposite direction to that in which he'd pointed and an extraordinary-looking vehicle came puttering around the bend of the lane. It was a huge open touring-car of the kind Jonathan associated with the twenties or thirties with a long bonnet, huge wheels and a very high body. It was the kind of car that really needed a chauffeur, but instead, there in the driving seat sat an equally extraordinary-looking old lady, very tall and thin with huge black eyes and an aristocratic looking beaky nose. She wore a long, flowing black dress.

The car juddered to a halt outside the station and stood shuddering, the engine still running. The old lady stared down at them, looking from the two men to Jonathan as if in puzzlement.

"I am looking for a young man called Jonathan Dent."

Jonathan stepped forward. "That's me."

The old lady looked at him as if he were something she'd ordered which didn't quite come up to standard. "I was expecting someone rather older."

Jonathan decided that if he was going to

spend a couple of weeks with this terrifying old bat, he'd better get things on the right footing from the start.

"I'm very sorry about my age," he said politely. "But I'm afraid there's not very much I can do about it."

The dark eyes flashed fiercely, and for a moment Jonathan wondered if he'd gone too far. Then the old lady smiled. "No, of course you can't," she said. "Do forgive me, you must think me very rude. I'm Caroline Boone, your great-aunt."

She held out her claw-like hand and Jonathan shook it. "How do you do, Great-Aunt Caroline?"

"Jump in," ordered the old lady briskly. "Put your luggage in the back and sit here beside me."

Jonathan obeyed.

The two businessmen had been watching this exchange in some astonishment. The younger of them stepped forward. "Miss Boone?"

The old lady looked down at him. "You have just heard me say so."

"Jack Potter, of Potter and Purbright. You

may remember we wrote to you."

"I am not in the habit of discussing my business affairs in the street, young man."

"I was wondering if we could come and see you."

"You may write to my lawyer for an appointment in the normal way. Now, if you will excuse me?"

Jack Potter seemed quite undeterred by his frosty reception. "I suppose you couldn't give us a lift to the inn could you? We're a bit stuck . . . "

'You suppose correctly," said the old lady acidly. "Unfortunately, I happen to be going in the opposite direction. The inn is only two miles down the road. By the look of you, the walk will do you good."

The car shot suddenly forwards, the old lady did a neat 'U' turn and rattled away.

As it rounded the bend, Jonathan turned and saw Potter and Purbright pick up their briefcases and suitcases and start trudging down the lane.

They looked tired already.

*　　*　　*

The old car put on a surprising turn of speed once it was moving, and it seemed to be going even faster in the narrow country lanes. Great-Aunt Caroline drove sitting bolt upright and glaring straight ahead, and somehow Jonathan knew that if anyone or anything appeared ahead, she would expect it to get out of her way. It probably would, too.

The speed and the noise made conversation difficult, and Jonathan guessed that the old lady probably disapproved of idle chatter. In addition she seemed to have something on her mind, and he heard her muttering something about "The vultures are gathering already."

He glanced back at the back seat to make sure his rucksack was okay, and saw Dave sitting beside it, clearly enjoying the ride. Dave winked and gave him a thumbs up sign, but to Jonathan's relief he made no attempt to speak.

The lane led them across flat green marshy fields with the sea beyond and eventually to the kind of old dark house in which Dracula would have felt quite at home. It managed to look sinister in the bright mid-day sunshine,

and Jonathan hated to think how it would
look on a dark and stormy night.

Great-Aunt Caroline drove the car up the
drive, past the front of the house, through an
archway into a cobbled yard, and finally into
an old stable, now obviously serving as a
garage.

Grabbing his rucksack – by now Dave had disappeared again – Jonathan followed the old lady through a back door into a big old stone-flagged kitchen, where a meal of bread and cheese and salad was set out on the wooden table. Great-Aunt Caroline waved towards it. "For you, young man."

Jonathan sat down at the table. "What about you?"

"At my age I subsist largely on tea and toast. I shall endeavour to provide some sort of evening meal, though I warn you, cooking isn't really one of my talents."

Jonathan started eating and Great-Aunt Caroline made a pot of tea, using a kettle which was simmering on an old-fashioned coal-burning cooker. She eventually pecked at a little bread and cheese herself, but only when Jonathan said he'd had enough.

Suddenly Jonathan realised that in this household food was probably in short supply.

"Mum gave me some money to put towards my food," he said casually.

"Certainly not, I wouldn't hear of it."

"I'll find the local shops and lay something in then," said Jonathan calmly.

For a moment the old lady glared fiercely at him, then her lips twitched. "You seem to be a very obstinate young man."

"Must run in the family," said Jonathan cheerfully. He was beginning to warm to his Great-Aunt. She was the sort of person who couldn't help trying to dominate everyone she met, and despised the ones who let her get away with it. The trick was not to stand any nonsense.

Which brought him to his next point. Polishing off the last of his salad, he took a swig of his cup of tea and looked thoughtfully at his Great-Aunt.

"Thanks very much for the meal," he said politely. "Now maybe you'll tell me why you've asked me down here."

CHAPTER THREE

The Summoning

Great-Aunt Caroline gave him the full benefit of her haughty stare.

"I should have thought my reasons were obvious enough."

"Such as?" said Jonathan encouragingly.

"A desire to see something of my family again, the wish for a little younger company, the hope of providing some deserving child with a little innocent pleasure . . ."

Jonathan burst out laughing. "I'm sorry but I don't believe a word of it."

"Well, really!" Great-Aunt Caroline rose in fury. "I am not accustomed to being spoken to in that manner."

"I'm sorry, I didn't mean to sound rude. But it really won't do, you know."

"What will not do?"

"These reasons of yours. According to my mum, you've done very well without seeing the family for years, and I bet if it was up to you you'd keep it that way. And as for wanting young children and giving some deserving child innocent pleasure – well, firstly you don't seem the type who'd want kids around, secondly, you obviously thought I was a lot older than I really am when you asked me."

Slowly Great-Aunt Caroline sat down. "I see you are intelligent as well as obstinate. You're quite right of course, I've been less than frank with you." She paused for a moment. "As you say, I've managed happily on my own for quite some time now. But recently things have become – difficult. It's become harder and harder to keep the house up on the little money I have left and there have been pressures from outside."

"What pressures?"

"Those two men who were on the train with you, Mr Potter and Mr Purbright . . . They're

33

property developers of some kind and they want to buy some sea-front land I own and . . . develop it."

"Sounds like the answer to all your problems."

Great-Aunt Caroline shuddered. "And ruin the whole area? My family have lived in the village for generations, and I still feel I have a duty towards it."

Jonathan frowned. "I can see how you might feel you needed some help – but why me?"

Great-Aunt Caroline looked puzzled. "I don't know. I just woke up one morning with the conviction that you, and you alone, were the one I needed. I had some vague idea you were much older, a lawyer or an accountant or something, though where I got it from heaven knows."

"Weird," said Jonathan briefly. He remembered his feeling on the train, that his journey had a purpose and that it was linked to his dream. "Well, what happens now?"

"I must confess I usually have a little sleep in the afternoons, but I scarcely imagine that you . . ."

Jonathan shook his head. "Not since I was about three anyway. I'd like to take a look around. Trouble is, you seem to be a bit of a way from anywhere. Didn't I see an old bike in your garage?"

She nodded. "It belonged to my nephew. It's been standing there ever since he – went away. I'm not sure if it's still in working order, though I've always looked after it."

Jonathan got up. "I'll take a look. Don't worry, I can always hoof it if I have to."

*   *   *

But the bike, when Jonathan inspected it, was in surprisingly good condition, almost as if it had spent the years in some bicycle museum. It was an ancient model with heavy tyres and solid mudguards, sit-up-and-beg handlebars and a carrier. The tyres were flat, but when they were pumped up they stayed up, and very soon Jonathan was wobbling down the drive towards the lane.

Great-Aunt Caroline had given him directions, and even drawn him a rough map. Left at the end of the drive took you straight to the village, right to the sea wall and the sea. Jonathan had worked out that if he turned right and rode to the sea wall and then left when he reached it, he could ride around the coast to the village and then take the direct route from the village back home.

After the lightweight, aluminium frame, drop handlebars sports model Jonathan was used to back home, the old bike felt like a tank but it got him along and by pedalling hard he was even able to get up a fair bit of speed.

A familiar voice spoke in his ear. "This is a bit of all right, isn't it?"

Glancing over his shoulder, he saw Dave perched on the carrier behind him.

"You're coming down in the world," said Jonathan. "First you were haunting a house, then a train and now a bike."

"I'm haunting you mate, and don't you forget it," said Dave. "Where are we off to anyway?"

Dave told him. "Weren't you around when I was in the kitchen?"

"No, I stayed outside. I don't like the feel of that house somehow. It's spooky."

Dave's presence on the bike didn't seem to make pedalling any harder – what did ghosts weigh after all, thought Jonathan – and the lane, like the fields around, was dead flat. Eventually they came to a brick wall almost hiding a cluster of weathered huts, topped by a rusty barbed-wire fence.

"That must be the old airfield," said Jonathan.

Dave leaped off the bike. "Right, let's go and take a look."

Leaning the bike against the wall, they walked into the airfield and stood looking around. They were in the middle of the little group of huts that had once been the airport buildings, and in the distance stretched the flat green fields that had once been the airstrip.

Suddenly Jonathan saw a group of young men sprawled outside the huts, some on deck-chairs, some on old wooden chairs dragged outside, others on the ground. Some of them wore flying suits and heavy sheepskin jackets, others were in their shirtsleeves. One of them looked up and stared hard at him.

"Looks as if the place isn't disused after all,"

said Jonathan. "Some local flying club must have taken it over. Surely they're in uniform, though . . ."

Dave didn't answer, and when Jonathan turned round, Dave wasn't even there . . .

Suddenly there was a whistling scream and one of the huts close to the edge of the field exploded in smoke and flame.

The roaring of engines filled the air and a loud voice crackled over the loudspeaker system. "Scramble, scramble, scramble! All pilots to their aircraft immediately. Airfield under attack!"

More bombs whistled down and the pilots leaped to their feet and began running towards the planes parked at intervals along the airfield.

Jonathan joined in the desperate stampede with the rest. He just had to get to his Spitfire and get airborne. A plane on the ground was a sitting target and squadrons had been destroyed that way. They were stretched desperately thin as it was, and couldn't afford to waste a single plane or a single pilot . . . Some fool was getting in his way, holding him back. A voice was calling, "Jonathan, Jonathan, come back . . . " The funny thing was, Jonathan wasn't even his name. He wished it was, better than a damn silly name like Tristram. Thank heaven none of the others knew the truth . . .

"Jonathan, come back, it's not safe," yelled the voice.

Jonathan felt a sort of mental tug, and suddenly he was standing in the middle of the quiet, deserted airfield, with Dave shaking him by the arm.

Jonathan stared dazedly at him. "What happened?"

"You tell me, mate. You just went away from me."

Jonathan told him what he'd seen and felt.

It was clear that Dave was badly shaken. "You went *back*," he whispered. "Back to their time, to the Battle of Britain. You mustn't do that, mate, it's too dangerous."

"I didn't exactly have much choice. I was suddenly *there*."

"You were summoned," said Dave solemnly. "Drawn there . . . Someone from the past *wants* you there . . . "

"Why did you say it was dangerous?"

"Because you were out of your body, weren't you? For a time, you were a ghost, like me."

"But my body was still alive, *here*. And I'm all right now."

"You're all right because you got back – because I called you back."

"Suppose I hadn't?" asked Jonathan. "Got back, I mean?"

"You'd have been stuck in that time forever."

"And what about the rest of me, that bit that was still here?"

"If you take the soul from a body, you're left with a sort of zombie. After a bit the body just withers and dies." Dave's voice was urgent. "Listen mate, if they try to pull you back there again, you've got to fight it."

"Hang on a minute," objected Jonathan. "You took me back to your own time once."

"You were dreaming, that time, and I was looking after you. This is different. Different, and dangerous . . . "

"I actually seemed to be someone else while it was happening," said Jonathan slowly. "Someone called Tristram."

Dave stared at him in horror. "You were possessed," he whispered. "Crikey, it's worse than I thought."

Jonathan shivered, suddenly cold in the blazing sun. "Let's get away from here."

They scrambled through the barbed wire and Jonathan heaved the old bike upright, and pedalled away from the airfield as fast as he could.

*   *   *

Some time later he was pedalling along the

43

path on top of the sea wall with water on both sides of him.

The water on his right was the sea and on his left was an enormous long, thin lake, a sort of lagoon. The whole coast was peaceful and deserted, and Jonathan found it hard to remember his recent terrifying experience. After all, midnight, not daylight was the time for ghosts. A phrase drifted into his mind, "The ghost in the mid-day sun . . . "

He turned to Dave who was back on the carrier. "What's going on then, Dave? Why me?"

"Search me, mate." Dave's voice was unusually serious. "That's what you've got to find out. I reckon that ghost, the other one I mean, wants something from you."

"But what?"

Dave shrugged. "Like I said, it wants something. And until you find out what it is and do it, it'll keep after you."

"Can't you help me?"

What was the use of having a resident ghost, thought Jonathan, if it couldn't help you out in a spot of bother with its fellow spooks?

Dave said, "I'll try. But it's dangerous, even for me."

"Why?"

"Look, I'm here because I want to be, right? But some ghosts are on earth because they *have* to be. They're tied to earth by some grudge, some piece of unfinished business. They spend years brooding on whatever's bothering them, and well, they can go a bit crazy. A really powerful one can just — wipe you out . . . "

They came to the turn-off that led down into the village.

*　　*　　*

There wasn't a lot to see in the village – a shop that sold everything you could ever possibly want, a garage and a pub, all grouped round a stagnant pond with a few dispirited ducks.

Jonathan visited the shop first, using the money his mother had given him to stock up with a variety of packets and cans and a few bottles as well. The results of his shopping filled up two large plastic bags which he lashed like saddlebags, one each side of the carrier on his bike.

The cycling and the shopping had made him thirsty, so he decided to explore the possibilities of the village pub.

Jonathan leaned his bike against the wall and went inside the cool dark bar. It was empty except for an old rustic in the corner sipping his pint, and a plump, motherly-looking lady behind the bar.

Before the lady could tell him he was too young to be in the pub Jonathan said, "Do you think I could have a coke or a lemonade or something? I'm dying of thirst."

"You can have a lemonade with pleasure, my love," said the landlady. "Only you'll have to drink it outside, 'cos of the licensing laws, see. You go and sit outside and I'll bring it, all right?"

Jonathan paid for his drink and went outside, sitting at one of the unoccupied tables.

The landlady came out with his lemonade. She looked at his bike. "Having a cycling holiday, my dear?"

"Well, not exactly," said Jonathan, grinning at the thought of touring on that iron monster. "I'm staying in the village for a bit – with my Great-Aunt Caroline, up at the house."

The landlady was impressed. "Well now, fancy that. She never has no company usually. Not like the old days. Once upon a time there was always people up at the big house but that's long gone." She rattled on a bit about the good old days when, apparently, the house had been the social centre of their countryside for miles around.

"Course, that's all finished now," she said sadly. "House parties and dances and shooting parties there was, so my mum used to tell me . . . "

"Were you here during the war?" asked Jonathan. "When there were fighters at the airfield?"

The landlady sighed. "That I was. Mind you I was only a little girl then. I used to help my mum collecting glasses, and washing up behind the bar."

Her eyes widened, as she stared back into the past. "We used to be crowded every night, then. Short life and a merry one the pilots used to say – and it was short enough for some of those poor boys. You know what they used to do?"

"No, what?"

"Well, they'd come in in little groups, like, little gangs of pals. And every now and again, you'd notice one of the group wasn't there any more. He was . . . missing. But the rest would all be quite cheerful – and they'd still buy the missing one a drink. They'd buy him his usual, and that drink would be just left there on the bar. And there it'd stay, all the evening, no-one would mention it, no-one would touch it. End of the evening they'd all pile into their old cars and roar back to the base. And a few nights later there was another one missing, another untouched drink on the bar . . . "

She smiled sadly. "Still, you don't want to hear all that, young lad like you. Terrible the way we old folk do go on about the war . . . "

"No, it's very interesting," said Jonathan. "Really, I mean it."

. . . And suddenly he was in a smoky, noisy bar, crowded with blue uniformed figures, laughing and chatting, and shouting orders for more drinks. Over in the corner a jolly group was singing.

Bless 'em all
Bless 'em all
The long and the short and the tall . . .

Jonathan was standing near the bar, but he wasn't one of the noisy, happy crowd. For some reason he was . . . apart.

A plump, pretty young woman was serving drinks, while from behind the bar a big-eyed, long-haired little girl surveyed the scene as she rinsed glasses in a sink.

A pilot officer with a ginger moustache was

buying a round of drinks.

"Five pints of bitter, a gin and tonic, and a brandy and soda."

He put the drinks on a battered tin tray, then added, "Oh yes, and another bitter for Tom." When the drinks arrived, the ginger-moustached pilot put the extra bitter carefully on the bar. Then looking straight at – no, straight through Jonathan he said, "Well, cheers Tom. There was no time to get to know

you, but you seemed like a pretty good type."
Raising a hand in farewell, he picked up the
tray and turned away.

Jonathan, though of course he wasn't
Jonathan any more, reached out a hand for
the drink – his drink. But his shadowy hand
passed right through the glass . . .

CHAPTER FOUR

The Deal

Somewhere far away, a voice was calling, "Jonathan! Come back, come back . . . "

He heard Dave's voice in his mind. "You've got to fight it . . . fight it . . . fight it . . . "

Jonathan made a mighty effort to remember not only where but who he was – and suddenly he was standing outside the pub in the hot sunshine with the landlady looking at him in concern.

"You all right, love? You looked miles away for a moment."

"I think I was," said Jonathan. "Or rather, years away."

The landlady looked baffled and Jonathan

said, "I'm all right, honestly, I just came over dizzy for a moment, must be the heat."

"It's my fault, keeping you out here chatting in the sun. Not often I get a chance to talk about the old days. No-one remembers, now, no-one wants to know. Just me and the old Wingco."

"Wingco?"

"The Wing Commander. He was here when the old field was still a fighter base, in the Battle of Britain. He liked the place so much he came back here to retire."

"I'd like to meet him," said Jonathan politely.

The landlady looked inside the pub at the clock over the bar. "He'll be here for his late lunchtime pint pretty soon. You'll see him if you hang on."

"Can't wait, I'm afraid, I've got to be getting back. Another day, maybe."

Jonathan was still feeling shaken and he was keen to get away. But it was too late.

A slim silver-haired old gentleman in a Royal Air Force blazer strode up to the pub.

"There you are, Wingco," said the landlady delightedly. "This young gentleman is interested in the old days, when the fighters were at the airfield."

"Is he indeed?" The old gentleman rubbed his hands. "Is he indeed? I'll have my usual pint, my dear, and if your young friend will join me in his usual tipple, I'll be glad to tell him all he wants to know."

Jonathan was trapped.

A few minutes later they were sitting at one of the tables, drinking beer and lemonade respectively.

"Right my lad," said the Wingco, after his first swig of beer. "We'll start with a bit of potted history. How much do you know about the Battle of Britain?"

"Not as much as I should, sir, I'm afraid."

The Wingco took another sip of beer. "Right! It's summer 1940 and Britain's losing the war. In fact Hitler says we've already lost and just haven't realised it yet. British Army's been defeated in France, what's left evacuated from Dunkirk."

"So things were looking pretty black?"

"Couldn't be blacker. Hitler's conquered France, Belgium, Holland. He's made himself the Master of Europe – except for us. Now, what's Hitler's next step?"

Jonathan jumped. "Er – invade England?"

"Exactly. Operation Sealion, plan to invade England all worked out – but . . . " The Wingco pointed seawards. "One major problem – out there."

That was an easy one. "The Channel," said Jonathan.

Next to Jonathan, though invisible to the Wingco, sat Dave listening in fascination to the story of events he'd lived through.

"Right," said the Wingco again. "Invasion by sea tricky business. German Navy, German Army, say can't be done unless —" This time he pointed upwards. Jonathan thought hard. "Unless Germany controlled the air?"

"Precisely." The Wingco seemed delighted at having found such a bright pupil. "Whereupon Goering . . ."

"He was the fat one wasn't he?" asked Jonathan.

"Exactly! Fat chap in a sky-blue uniform, in charge of the German Air Force. 'Leave it to me', says fatty, 'my brave lads will drive the British from the skies.'"

At this point Dave blew a hearty raspberry.

The Wingco frowned, like someone who hears a distant noise. "Sorry, did you say something?"

"No, no," said Jonathan, scowling at Dave to shut up.

"Anyway," the Wingco went on, "that was the Battle of Britain. Went on right through the summer of 1940. They sent their fighters and bombers over day by day, we fought back

with everything we'd got. Short of planes, short of pilots, short of everything. One big advantage, Radar! We could usually see the blighters coming, put our planes where they were needed."

He took another swig of beer. "End of the day, we won, or at least, we didn't lose. Goering never got command of the air, Germany never invaded. Hitler keeps postponing Sealion, finally goes off the whole idea, and attacks Russia instead. Damnfool idea, probably lost him the war, that and the Yanks coming in on our side."

Suddenly a voice interrupted them. "I say, have you got a minute?" A young man in grey flannels and an open-necked shirt was standing in the pub doorway.

For a moment Jonathan didn't recognise him. Then he saw it was one of the two businessmen he'd met on the train. He looked a lot less stuffy in his casual gear, and his manner was a good deal more friendly.

"I'd very much like us to have a little chat if you could spare me a moment." The request was made so charmingly it was impossible to refuse, and besides, Jonathan was curious as to what was behind it.

"Okay," he said obligingly. He turned to the Wingco, "Goodbye sir."

The young man said, "Jolly good, let's have a drink on it, shall we? What'll you have?"

"How about a Vodka Martini, shaken and not stirred?" The young man gaped and Jonathan said hurriedly, "Sorry, too many James Bond movies, another lemonade will do fine."

"Splendid. A dry sherry for me and a lemonade for my friend."

When they were sitting at another of the

outside tables with their drinks the young man held out his hand. "Jack Potter, of Potter and Purbright. You met my partner, old Freddie. Bit of a twit, to be honest, but loads of contacts."

Jonathan shook hands. "Jonathan Dent."

"I'm afraid we got off on the wrong foot rather, earlier on. Apologies and all that." Jack Potter grinned. "To be honest, if we'd known who you were, we'd have treated you with a lot more respect. Your Great-Aunt is very important to us right now."

"Why?" asked Jonathan bluntly.

"Freddy and I are developers in a small way, just starting up on our own. We've got this really splendid scheme for a marina. This is the deal . . . "

*   *   *

"So what's a marina?" asked Dave, now back on the carrier as Jonathan cycled home.

"Sort of a specially built harbour for small boats, pleasure yachts and that sort of thing. Boating's very big these days."

Dave said wonderingly, "Yachts! In my day

most people didn't even have cars."

"Anyway," said Jonathan, "these two characters have got it all worked out but they can't start without a strip of sea-front land Great-Aunt Caroline owns, just by that lagoon we saw."

"And she won't sell to them?"

"She won't even talk to them. She reckons it goes against her obligations to the village or something."

"So where do you come in?"

"I said I'd try and get her at least to listen to them . . . though whether she'll listen to me . . . "

Great-Aunt Caroline was up and pottering around the garden when Jonathan got back, and since she seemed quite happily occupied, Jonathan spent the afternoon exploring, first the huge rambling garden, and then the big old house. There were scores of rooms, most of them unused. The one he was to sleep in had a four-poster bed, velvet curtains and lots of heavy oak furniture. Jonathan was afraid it would be like sleeping in a museum.

"A house like this is really worth haunting," said Dave, materialising suddenly and bouncing on the bed. "None of your modern rubbish."

"Why not take it over?"

Suddenly serious, Dave said, "Because there's someone here already."

"Another ghost, you mean?"

Dave nodded. "I could feel it the minute we came in."

"What sort of a ghost?" asked Jonathan, a little nervously. "A friendly one, like you?"

Dave shook his head. "I doubt it, somehow.

I'm doing my best to track it down . . . "

And with that he vanished.

*   *   *

When Great-Aunt Caroline came in from the garden, she found Jonathan in the kitchen preparing supper.

"Sausages, eggs and chips," he said, "basic but nourishing. Just you sit down and leave it all to me."

The old lady obeyed. "Things have certainly changed. In my days, young men expected to be waited on."

"You'd wait a long time to be waited on in our house," said Jonathan. "Mum works all kinds of odd hours, so Dad and I have learned to cope by ourselves."

During supper, Jonathan told her about his meeting with Jack Potter.

The old lady shuddered. "Vultures!" she said. "As I said before, it goes against all my sense of obligation to the village."

"You know," said Jonathan thoughtfully, "I'm not so sure you haven't got it all wrong."

"Got it wrong!" hissed Great-Aunt

Caroline, looking as if she was about to turn him into a toadstool any minute.

Jonathan nodded. "I mean, in the good old days, this house must have meant a lot in the life of the village. Jobs for servants and gardeners and gamekeepers and heaven knows what, money spent on food for all those house parties . . . "

"Go on."

"Well, what can you do for them now?"

"Nothing," said the old lady bitterly. "Death and taxes have reduced me to a state where I can hardly look after myself, let alone help others."

"This marina," said Jonathan. "It would mean lots of jobs when it was being built, lots of jobs when it was going too. Boat building and repair, work on engines, sail-making, not to mention jobs in the yacht club that goes with it. It could bring the village back to life."

"I will not have the whole village ruined," said the old lady furiously.

"Who's talking about ruining it? Nice little harbour with yachts in it, a few well-designed buildings. You could be on the Board of Directors, keep them all in order . . . "

But it was no use. Great-Aunt Caroline refused to even think about the marina proposition, and wouldn't even consider meeting Potter and Purbright.

Jonathan decided to leave it at that. He had no particular reason to do Potter and Purbright any favours, though he genuinely thought the proposed marina could be a very good thing, both for the village and for Great-Aunt Caroline herself. Not only would it provide her with some much needed income, it would give her something new to think about. Jonathan had already realised that she spent much of her time brooding over the tragedies of the past.

After supper she picked up the big oil lamp and led Jonathan along gloomy corridors to the portrait gallery.

The shadows of the old house seemed to press in on the flickering lamp.

"Did you ever think about putting in electricity?" asked Jonathan.

"Oh yes, we were pioneers. We used to have our own generator. Unfortunately it broke down years ago, and I can't afford to have it repaired."

In the portrait gallery, family portraits sprang out of the darkness. Men in armour, men in doublet and hose, bewhiskered dignitaries in the colourful uniforms and sober frock-coats of the Victorian age . . .

The old lady lingered longest on the uniformed portraits at the far end of the long gallery, and Jonathan realised that these were people she had actually known. "My father and all my uncles were lost in the First World War. I lost my three brothers and the man I was going to marry in World War Two."

Jonathan didn't know what to say. "They must have been very brave."

"They were heroes," said the old lady bitterly. "They were heroes and now they are dead. Be thankful you won't have to give your life for a patch of African desert or a few yards of trampled French mud."

"Yes, it's different now," said Jonathan. "We'll all go together when we go."

He pointed to a blank space at the end of the line of portraits. "There seems to be room for just one more."

"That space was intended for my nephew, the only male survivor on my side of the family. But his portrait will never hang there."

"Why not?"

The old lady was silent for a moment. Then she said, "He was always wild and reckless. What they used to call a rake, always in trouble, drink, women, gambling. He had great charm though, and usually managed to talk his way out of trouble. Many a time I paid his debts, gave him a fresh start."

"So what happened to him?"

"We quarrelled bitterly at the beginning of

the war. He refused to join up, said he didn't want to join the long line of dead heroes. I told him he was a disgrace to the family, gave him money for the last time and he went away. I never saw him again. I heard he'd gone to Canada, and on to America – they were neutral then."

Suddenly Jonathan's dream flooded back into his mind. "Was his name Tristram?"

A gust of wind rushed through the gallery, slamming a loose shutter against the wall and almost blowing out the oil lamp.

The old lady shielded it with her hand. She stared at Jonathan in amazement.

"That's right . . . But how could you know that? My nephew's name was Tristram . . . Tristram Boone."

*   *   *

That night Jonathan lay awake in the big four-poster, looking at the flickering candle that he didn't quite like to blow out.

Suddenly Dave appeared on the end of the bed. "You ought to get out of here, mate, soon as you can. Tomorrow, better still tonight."

"Why?"

"This place isn't safe not for you. It's haunted."

"Of course it's haunted," said Jonathan. "You're here."

"I don't mean haunted by me," said Dave fiercely. "I mean really haunted, by one of those earth-bound spirits I told you about — that possessed you this afternoon. Something really powerful – and it's coming for you."

Jonathan drew a deep breath. "So what do I do?"

"Stay awake, mate. Sit up all night. And if it does appear, don't go with it. I only just got you back twice today and the pull's much stronger now. If you get trapped on the Other Side . . . "

Jonathan shuddered. "I know. I'll be a ghost like you. A ghost from the future."

Suddenly the candle blew out and the door flew open.

A young man in flying clothes stood in the doorway. It was one of the young men Jonathan had seen at the airfield that afternoon, the one who'd stared at him.

The figure beckoned.

"No," whispered Dave. "Don't go. Remember what I told you."

Jonathan felt not only a pull but a sort of desperate appeal coming from the figure in the doorway. "I've got to go with him, Dave. He needs help. Might as well get it over with."

"No!" shouted Dave.

Ignoring him, Jonathan lay back and closed his eyes. Immediately he felt himself drawn away . . .

Suddenly he was back on the airfield, scrambling desperately to reach his plane.

This time he let himself be swept forward with the others.

"Scramble! Scramble! Scramble!" squawked the tannoy. "Airfield under attack." Jonathan pounded across the grass and climbed into the cockpit of his Spitfire.

The corporal mechanic was standing by, and helped to strap him in. He pulled down the transparent canopy, and made a rapid instrument check. With automatic skill his hands moved over the controls and the Merlin engines coughed into life.

He waved to the corporal who jumped off the wing and pulled the chocks from under the wheels. Jonathan, or rather the Spitfire pilot Jonathan had become, opened the throttle and the plane jolted across the grass and seemed to leap into the sky.

As always it swung a little on take-off, but he soon had it trimmed. Came off the ground pretty sharpish, the old Spitfire, he thought.

And you could see all around you too, thanks to the transparent canopy. He checked the weaponry, eight Browning machine-guns, four housed in each wing . . .

Almost immediately, the machine-guns came into use.

The enemy were up in force, and he found himself above a Dornier bomber, one of those attacking the field. Screaming down he raked it again and again with machine-gun fire. The Dornier staggered, sending out streams of smoke, but it didn't go down. Built like flying tanks, those Dorniers . . .

Still it was crippled and had to turn for home.

Immediately he was engaged with one of the Messerschmidt BF 109 s that formed the bomber escort.

Switching on the reflector sight and turning the safety catch back to 'fire' position he opened the throttle and sped straight towards the enemy. He opened fire at almost point-blank range, and a spray of oil on his windscreen showed him the Messerschmidt was hit.

Glancing down, he saw it spinning towards the ground giving out a thick trail of smoke.

All around the air seemed full of planes, the attacking bombers and their Messerschmidt fighter escorts. The bombers of course were the main target, but each bomber was protected by fighters.

With a savage burst of fire he blew the canopy from an attacking Messerschmidt, and as he shot by he saw the white canopy of its pilot's parachute drifting towards the ground.

Swooping up on another enemy fighter from below he blew up the tail unit with an accurate burst of fire.

Suddenly he became aware of an enemy fighter on his tail. He sideslipped to port and then to starboard, but the fighter still hung on.

He flicked over into a stall-turn, raking the enemy with his machine-guns as the Messerschmidt flashed by sideways-on, presenting an unmissable target.

The Messerschmidt burst into flames and went down in a flat spin, exploding as it hit the ground.

And so the afternoon went on as the Spitfires made darting attacks at the lumbering bombers, and fought savage one-to-one battles *with their fighter escorts . . .*

His final battle came just as the day was ending.

He spotted another BF 109, just coming out of its turn a few thousand yards ahead. The German saw him at the same time and spun towards him, attacking head on.

Peering through his reflector sight he opened fire, and the Messerschmidt fired at the same time. He could feel the bullets thudding into the Spitfire and the BF 109 was so close it looked as if they must crash. At the last minute he looped first under and then up and over the Messerschmidt, diving down out of the setting sun and raking the enemy from above.

The Messerschmidt went into a spin, spiralling downwards streaming smoke. A numbness in his side and the faltering in his engine told him that both he and his Spitfire were badly damaged.

In the failing light, he struggled to regain the airfield. The engines cut out and the Spitfire glided silently downwards . . .

Both the light and his own sight were failing now, and he was flying into a silvery haze.

There below him was a long smooth stretch of grass. Was it his field, or some other? No matter, it was the perfect spot for an emergency landing . . .

He made a final effort and brought the

plane into land.

It was only as his wheels were about to touch down that he realised that the ground below wasn't ground at all . . .

* * *

Jonathan was himself again, but that self was lost, floating in misty nothingness.

He shuddered, remembering Dave's warnings. Was he trapped here forever, doomed to float in this limbo, while his real body withered and died . . . ?

He was gripped by a sensation of overpowering terror. He felt literally paralysed by fear.

Suddenly he saw a glowing figure just ahead.

A tall young man in pilot's uniform. The figure beckoned, and Jonathan followed . . .

CHAPTER FIVE

Homecoming

Jonathan awoke.

Someone was shaking his shoulder.

Not his mum, not Dave . . .

He opened his eyes and saw Great-Aunt Caroline glaring indignantly down at him. "I know you are on holiday, young man, but I really felt I had to wake you. It's past mid-day."

Jonathan blinked. "Sorry, I've had rather a tiring night. I'll get up now."

"So I should hope."

As the old lady stomped off a frantic Dave materialised. "You're back! I've been searching for you, but I couldn't find you.

How did you manage it?"

"*He* brought me back, Dave, the pilot. I know what he wants me to do now."

"What is it?"

Jonathan shook his head. "Not yet. If my theory's right you'll see in good time, and so will everyone else." He jumped out of bed. "I need a bit more information before I'm completely sure. And I know just the man to give it to me . . . "

* * *

The Wingco was sitting in front of the pub with his pint when Jonathan pedalled up.

He seemed delighted to see him. "Come for another ear-bashing, my lad? You're a glutton for punishment, you are. Still, they were glorious days, you know. We stood alone, defying the Nazi hordes!"

Dave appeared and gave a cheer, and Jonathan said hurriedly, "And you were here throughout the Battle of Britain, at the airfield?"

"Yes, indeed. Only a small field, mind, but we did our bit. I could tell you some tales . . . "

And so he did, going on for quite a while.

When the flow of stories looked like tailing off, Jonathan said, "I'm interested in one particular pilot actually. I don't know if you knew him."

"Knew 'em all," said the Wingco. "What was his name?"

"That's the problem, I don't know. I can tell you what he looked like, tall, thin-faced, dark eyes. I don't think he was with you very long. He probably got shot down soon after he arrived."

"So did quite a few of them," said the Wingco sadly. "We were using pilots without proper experience towards the end, all we'd got. Lads fresh out of flying school, and a cut-down course at that. Quite a few didn't last very long."

Suddenly Jonathan remembered going back in time to the crowded bar. "A bitter for Tom," the pilot had said.

"I can tell you his first name – Tom. He used to drink bitter."

The Wingco gazed into space as if picturing long-vanished faces. Then he pounded his fist on the table. "Tom Brown!"

Just the sort of nice ordinary name he'd choose, thought Jonathan. Out loud he said, "That sounds like the one. What happened to him?"

"Poor old Tom Brown," said the Wingco sadly. "Came to us straight from flying school in Canada – a lot of our pilots trained over there. Good looking young devil, liked a drink and a laugh . . . "

Jonathan was more and more certain he'd got the right man. "What happened?" he asked again.

"He was with us three days. Then he vanished. Missing in action."

"How did it happen?"

"It was the day they decided to hit our airfield. Came over just as we were ready to take off. Heck of a dogfight, went on all day. Somewhere in the middle of it all, young Tom Brown vanished. Someone said they'd seen him down a Messerschmidt near the end of the day, but after that he just disappeared. Radar was out, communications out, anything could have happened. Went down in the drink, most likely."

Perhaps, thought Jonathan. Or perhaps . . .

He jumped up. "Thanks a lot for the talk, sir. Now there's someone I've got to see." He ran into the inn and bumped into Jack Potter coming down the stairs. "The very man," said Jonathan breathlessly. "Now listen, I may be able to get Great-Aunt Caroline interested. Suppose I persuade her to talk to you, and maybe even make some kind of deal."

Jack Potter gave him a slap on the back that nearly knocked him over.

"That would be terrific!"

"But if she does, you've got to promise to do something."

"Like what?"

Jonathan told him.

Jack Potter said, "But we'd have had to do that anyway. The foundations for the harbour . . . "

"I know," said Jonathan. "I just want you to do it sooner rather than later."

They talked for a while longer, then Jack said, "Okay! You get the old dear to sign on the dotted line, and it's a deal."

As Jonathan pedalled furiously back to the house, he heard Dave's voice in his ear. "Look, what do you think you're up to, mate?"

"You'll see," said Jonathan. "If I can only persuade Great-Aunt Caroline, you'll all see."

"See what?"

"The answer to a mystery – nearly fifty years old . . . "

* * *

Jonathan's whole scheme nearly came a cropper over Great-Aunt Caroline.

"Certainly not!" said the old lady furiously. "I've already told you, I won't hear of it. My responsibility is to the village."

"Seems to me your responsibility is to

bring the place to life, not sit by and watch it die slowly. And they're offering a wonderful deal . . . A seat on the board for you, and a handsome salary. You'd have final say on all the designs . . . "

Jonathan had to talk himself hoarse before the old lady would grudgingly consent to at least meet and talk with the developers.

And of course, it didn't help at all that he couldn't possibly tell her the real reason why he was so keen for the deal to go through . . .

*   *   *

It was dawn, the lowest of low tide a couple of days later. Jonathan, Jack Potter and Freddie Purbright and Great-Aunt Caroline were all standing on the sea wall between the sea and the lagoon, just close to the airfield. The Wingco was there as well, and so was Dave, although no-one but Jonathan could see him.

It had taken a lot of talk and negotiation and deal-making to get them all here, and Jonathan only hoped it was going to be worth it.

"It's basically a simple enough process," Jack Potter was saying. "We blow out a chunk of sea wall at low tide, and the lagoon drains out onto the sands. We reckon that'll take less than an hour. That gives us a couple of hours to repair the damage so the sea can't flood back in. Everyone ready?"

No one said they weren't so Jack Potter waved a signal to a hard-hatted figure some way along the wall.

The man waved back, bent over a black box and seconds later there was a *crump* sound and a spurt of earth and sand from a point in the sea wall half-way between him and them.

"How disappointing," said Great-Aunt Caroline. "I was expecting something far more spectacular."

"We want to breach the sea wall, not blow it up," said Jack Potter. "Water pressure will do most of the work for us."

For a time it seemed nothing was happening.

Then they saw lagoon water flooding out over the sands, and slowly the water level in the lagoon started to fall.

As it fell, a shape began to appear from

beneath the water.

First the tail, then part of the fuselage, then a wing-tip . . .

They watched in amazement as the shape of the complete plane was finally revealed. "What on earth . . . " whispered Great-Aunt Caroline. "What is it?"

"It's the last Spitfire," said Jonathan. "Flown by your vanished nephew, Tristram Boone."

* * *

"You see he must have listened to you after all," said Jonathan. "Instead of going to America he stayed in Canada and enlisted in a flying school under the name of Tom Brown."

They were all sitting in the private parlour of the inn, drinking coffee supplied by the astonished landlady.

"Then, of course, he got posted to this airfield, right next to your house."

Great-Aunt Caroline was still dazed. "But why didn't he come and see me?"

"I expect he would have," said Jonathan.

"He'd only been there a few days, remember. Maybe he wanted to do something to make you proud of him before he turned up."

"Well, he certainly did that," said the old lady softly.

The Wingco said, "And he was trying to get back to base, probably wounded with his plane damaged and he made it just as far as the lagoon."

Jack Potter shook his head. "Amazing. How did you work all this out, young fellow?"

"Oh, luck and guesswork," said Jonathan vaguely.

After all, there was no way he could tell them the truth.

Great-Aunt Caroline said sadly, "And now I can have his portrait painted at last – and hang it in the gallery with my other dead heroes."

*   *   *

It wasn't until very much later that Jonathan could talk about what had really happened. And, of course, the only one he could talk to was Dave.

They sat together on a deserted stretch of the sea wall, watching the crowd gathering round the Spitfire on the lagoon bed. Already the police had roped the plane off, and the pilot's body had been taken away. Eventually Tristram Boone's body would lie in the local churchyard beside his ancestors, and, Jonathan hoped, his spirit would finally be at rest.

"I'm still not sure how I got drawn in to all this," he said.

Dave said importantly, "I reckon it was because of me."

"Why you?"

"Well poor old Tristram couldn't get through to the old girl, see. She's the sort that won't believe in ghosts and never sees them.

But when you and I met, I reckon that somehow he managed to get to know about you."

"On the ghosts' grapevine, you mean?"

"I am talking about the astral plane, mate," said Dave with dignity. "Don't mock. Anyway, he was able to plant the idea of sending for you in the old girl's mind when she was asleep. Then when you turned up, he used you to get the truth brought to light. You did a good job there, mate."

"So I've got you to thank, have I?" said Jonathan. "As if it isn't bad enough to get haunted once, I get haunted twice."

Dave gave him a reproachful look. "Come off it mate, you ought to be grateful! How many kids can say they've flown a Spitfire in the Battle of Britain?"

"How many people can I tell about it?" asked Jonathan.

"I don't know," said Dave. "Some people are never satisfied."

"Come on," said Jonathan. "Let's take a closer look at my plane."

The School Spirit

CHAPTER ONE

The Haunted Bus

'Here we go, here we go, here we go!' sang the coach-load of schoolkids happily. 'Here we go, here we go, here we go-oo! Here we go, here we go, here we go! Here we go-o, here we go!'

Jonathan turned to his friend, a small bespectacled boy called Timothy. 'I'm not mad about the words – or the tune either come to that.'

Timothy, a keen musician, nodded. 'It's got a certain rhythmic force. But as a musical statement, it definitely lacks variety.'

'Here we go, here we go, here we go!'

carolled their schoolmates cheerfully, launching into the umpteenth chorus.

Jonathan grinned. 'Well, at least they're enjoying themselves.'

'And driving the teachers crazy at the same time,' pointed out Timothy. 'Sort of a fringe benefit.'

Jonathan nodded thoughtfully. 'Can't be bad! Shall we?'

He and Timothy raised their voices. 'Here we go, here we go, here we go . . .'

They were sitting at the back of the specially-hired mini bus on the way to a school weekend trip.

Most schools run something of the kind. A mixed group of pupils and teachers spend a weekend at some country retreat. There's a bit of study, a bit of sport and a lot of messing about. No-one's quite sure what it's supposed to achieve, but people seem to enjoy it.

Most people, that is.

Mr Fox, Jonathan's form master, was sitting in the front seat next to the art master, a fiery Welshman called Huw Hughes.

Mr Fox was red-haired, thin faced and at

the moment, a picture of gloom. 'What beats me is the way I keep volunteering each year. Like the victim signing on for another turn on the rack. Why do we do it, Huw? Why *do* we do it?'

'Well, I dunno about you, boyo. It's a combination of things with me. A chance to drink in the beauties of nature, the opportunity to watch keen young minds develop, and the beer in the village pub.'

'There is that,' agreed Mr Fox, cheering up. 'With any luck, we'll get there in time for a pint before closing time.'

'If we manage to find the place,' said Huw Hughes. 'New digs this time, remember.'

At the back of the coach, Timothy was explaining things to Jonathan who was fairly new at the school.

'I shall miss Farrow's Farm. Mrs Farrow's cooking was terrific.'

'Why the change?'

'Old Farmer Farrow retired and sold the place. The new owner said he "didn't want no blasted kids traipsing around".' Timmy said the last bit in a thick Mummerset accent.

'So where are we going then?'

'To the Old Manor House,' said Timmy impressively. 'The squire died just recently and the place went to some nephew from London. Apparently he's keen to make the Old Manor earn its keep, and when the school asked him about having us there he jumped at it.'

'Doesn't know what he's in for, does he? What's the place like?'

'Nobody knows. The old squire was pretty much a hermit, and he never let anyone inside the place. I think the Headmaster visited it when they signed the agreement. Apparently he said it was "interesting and picturesque".'

'Sounds – ouch!' yelled Jonathan.

The ouch was caused by a sharp sting on his ear. 'What's the matter?' asked Timothy. 'Insect bite?'

Jonathan picked a tightly-wadded V of paper from his lap. 'A human insect – with a good strong rubber band.'

Timothy looked at the row of seat-backs

ahead of them. 'Who, though?'

'I've a pretty good idea,' said Jonathan. 'Don't worry, he won't be able to resist having a gloat.'

Sure enough, a grinning face appeared round the back of a seat several rows ahead. A big hand appeared too, with a thick rubber band looped round one finger. 'All right, Jonno?'

It was Basher Briggs, the nearest thing they had to a school bully. He and Jonathan had tangled several times before, and somehow or other Briggs had always come off worst.

He was about to come off worst again.

Above Jonathan's head, a familiar voice said, 'Dear oh dear, some people never learn, do they?'

Jonathan looked up. Stretched out in the luggage rack above his head, using Jonathan's rucksack as a sort of pillow, was a boy of his own age. He wore baggy grey shorts held up by a cricket belt, a grey flannel shirt and grubby white tennis shoes.

It wasn't the way kids liked to dress today – but Dave wasn't exactly your everyday kid.

Dave was a ghost.

Way back in World War Two a robot-bomb, a buzz-bomb as they were known then, had hit the roof of his house, destroying Dave's attic bedroom and Dave as well.

The bomb damage had eventually been repaired and years later Jonathan's family had moved into the house. Jonathan soon discovered that Dave, or rather his ghost, was still very much around.

Once Jonathan had got over the shock, he and Dave had become good friends – best mates, as Dave put it. But Jonathan had soon discovered that having a ghost for a friend wasn't without problems.

Much of the time, Dave was around but invisible. Even when he was visible, like now, only Jonathan could see him – which meant Jonathan sometimes seemed to be talking to himself. But the real problem was that Dave insisted on being helpful – and Dave's help could be embarrassing to say the least. Jonathan had a terrible feeling Dave was going to be helpful now.

Jonathan stood up pretending to make sure his rucksack was secure. 'I'll deal with Briggsy later, Dave, don't make a fuss.'

'Don't worry, mate, discretion is our watchword.'

Dave vanished, leaving a ghostly chuckle behind.

Jonathan sat down resignedly. Something was going to happen – it was just a matter of when.

Dave's well-meaning efforts had already given Jonathan a bit of a reputation in school. Nothing specific, just a feeling that odd things seemed to happen when he was around. Jonathan hated it, and was desperately trying to live it down.

Now he sat staring up the aisle at where Briggs was sitting.

He almost missed it at first.

Something rose in the air from Briggsy's seat and hovered above it. It was a sort of circle, a loop . . .

It was a thick rubber band.

Hooked into the band was a piece of paper, folded many times into a sort of stubby V – one of Briggsy's missiles.

Rubber band and missile floated down the centre aisle of the bus – and hovered just behind the two teachers.

The band stretched into an oval, pulled back by the V – and the paper V shot forwards hitting Huw Hughes on the back of his neck.

He leaped to his feet and turned round with a roar of rage – just as Briggsy yelled and jumped up too, staring at the rubber band that was suddenly looped round his hand . . .

CHAPTER TWO
Dracula's Castle

Huw Hughes shot down the aisle, hauled Briggsy halfway out of his seat and shook him till his teeth rattled. 'Now just you listen to me, boyo! I know we relax the rules a bit on the school trip – but that does not entitle you to assault a teacher with a deadly weapon, understand?'

Briggs nodded dumbly. Dropping him back in his seat the still-seething teacher returned to the front of the bus.

'Wonder what got into old Briggsy?' said Timothy curiously.

Jonathan grinned. 'Got a bit over-confident, didn't he?'

Timmy looked thoughtfully at him. 'You know, Jonathan, it's a funny thing . . . '

Jonathan knew exactly what Timothy was going to say. Whenever anyone hassled Jonathan, somehow things always turned out badly for that person. It was just the sort of thinking he wanted to discourage.

To his relief there was a timely interruption. Mr Fox, who had been deep in conversation with the driver, turned round and shouted. 'Quiet a minute, you lot!'

'Foxy's going to make a speech,' said Jonathan.

Someone heard the last word and took it up. 'Speech, speech!' they shouted.

Mr Fox glared at his mutinous audience until they fell silent. 'We are now very close to the Old Manor House,' he began.

The announcement was greeted with cheers.

'However, since this is our first visit, no-one is sure exactly how to get there.'

There were boos and cries of 'Shame!' and 'Who organised this disaster anyway?'

Someone who'd been studying Politics shouted, 'Resign! Resign!'

Like the Prime Minister at Question Time, Foxy pressed on. 'We are therefore going to stop at the village pub, which we do know how to find . . . '

Shouts of 'I bet!' and more ironic cheers.

' . . . in order to get precise directions for the last stage of the journey,' Foxy concluded. 'Younger boys will remain outside. Hadley and Sutton and other sixth formers will collect refreshment orders and money from their fellows.'

Foxy sat down amidst more cheers and soon they were drawing up outside the little village pub which sat, like a Tourist Board poster, on the village green.

There were wooden benches and tables outside, and everyone jostled for a place while the sixth formers took endless orders for lemonade, coke and crisps.

Meanwhile, Foxy and Huw Hughes disappeared inside the bar to ask directions from the landlord and, everyone said knowingly, to sink a swift pint as well.

Jonathan and Timothy didn't bother with the wooden benches, and sat down on the grass by the front door, well-placed to grab two cokes when Hadley staggered past with a laden tray.

They were also well-placed to overhear the conversation when Huw Hughes and Foxy, both wiping their lips appreciatively, appeared in the doorway with a tubby balding man in an apron.

'Left down Manor Lane, then left again up Manor Drive,' he was saying. ''Tis powerful overgrown, you'll just about get that coach up, I reckon.' He paused. 'Excuse me, sir,

you're sure it's the *Old* Manor you want?'

'Pretty sure,' said Foxy. He fished a folded letter out of his pocket and showed it to the landlord. 'There you are, "The Old Manor House, Hobs Hollow." That's it, isn't it?'

The landlord peered at the letter. 'That's it, right enough. Only . . . the old squire never had anyone in the house, save that housekeeper of his. He wouldn't even have village folk there, let alone . . . '

'Let alone a parcel of juvenile hooligans from London?' said Huw Hughes cheerfully.

The landlord looked sheepish. 'Well now, sir . . . '

'The old squire's dead now though,' said Mr Fox briskly. 'The place has passed to his nephew, and he's very keen to have us – as you can see from his letter.'

The landlord shook his head. 'The old squire wouldn't have liked it when he was alive. Old Manor's got a bad reputation in these parts. It's unlucky for children. You could have chosen a better place to bring your boys, sir, and that's the truth. You'd do better to go back home.'

Still shaking his head, the landlord

disappeared into his pub. Foxy and Huw
Hughes exchanged astonished glances, then
Foxy raised his voice. 'Back in the coach,
everyone!'

As Jonathan stood up, he was about to
follow the others when he felt a tap on his
shoulder. He turned and saw Dave standing
in the doorway.

'That was good advice, mate. I'd get your
teachers to take it if I were you.'

'What do you mean?'

'I've been getting bad feelings about this

Old Manor place – and they're getting stronger as we get nearer.'

'Bad vibrations on the spiritual plane?'

'You can take the mickey if you like, mate, but just be warned.'

And with that Dave vanished.

Jonathan went uneasily back to the coach. He'd learned quite a bit about the unseen world since meeting Dave. Not all Earthbound spirits were as harmless as his ghostly friend . . .

Soon they were on their way again, the coach jolting along ever-narrowing country lanes.

'You know what that business in the pub reminded me of ?' said Timothy.

Jonathan shook his head. 'No, what?'

'Those old Hammer horror movies they show on telly! They always start with some innocent young bloke turning up at the village inn and asking the way to Castle Dracula. And all the local peasants go "Aaargh! Don't 'ee go to Castle Dracula, young master!" And of course he never listens. Off he goes, and sooner or later – pow!'

'Well, what about it?'

'We're not listening either, are we?' Suddenly Timothy looked serious.

The coach lurched as they made a sharp right turn, and crawled up a lane so narrow that branches tapped the windows on either side.

'Heaven help us if we meet something going the other way,' said Timothy.

Jonathan said, 'Well, I wouldn't worry about it – it doesn't look as if anything's been along this lane for years and years.'

Suddenly the coach jolted to a stop. The driver, Mr Fox and Huw Hughes all got out, and everybody else poured out after them.

The coach was parked outside a set of massive iron gates. On the other side of the gates was a long gravel drive, and at the end of the drive was a sinister old building, towers and turrets rising black against the rapidly darkening sky.

'Looks as if you were right, Timothy,' whispered Jonathan. 'Dracula's Castle!'

Timothy looked horrified. 'We're not going in there, are we?'

'I doubt it. Look at those gates.'

The gates were held closed by a length of iron chain, ending in a huge rusty padlock.

Huw Hughes and Mr Fox stood staring at the gates in bafflement. There was no-one to be seen, and the house stood dark and silent.

Huw Hughes turned to the driver. 'Give 'em a toot, boyo!'

The driver honked his horn and the sound echoed all around them, shattering the evening hush.

But no-one came out to meet them. As Timothy went forward to look at the gate, Jonathan felt bony fingers gripping his arm.

He turned and saw that it was Dave, pulling him to one side.

'Listen mate,' hissed Dave fiercely. 'This is your chance.'

'Chance to what?'

'To get everyone out of here! Just you try and persuade those teachers of yours there's been some mix-up and you might as well all go home.'

'That's probably what'll happen anyway,' said Jonathan. 'Why are you so het up about it?'

'Because there's something evil, in that

house. Evil and angry – and hungry. It's been starved up till now because the place has been more or less empty. But if you lot turn up . . .'

'But the place is empty,' protested Jonathan. 'No-one seems to live there.'

'I wasn't talking about anyone alive,' said Dave, and disappeared.

CHAPTER THREE

Sinister Welcome

The two teachers stood staring at the locked gates.

'I just don't understand it,' said Mr Fox. 'The Head made the arrangements ages ago, and he got a letter of confirmation back from the new owner. Look, here it is.'

He produced the letter, the same one he'd shown the landlord of the pub.

'No use waving letters at me, boyo,' said Huw Hughes sourly. 'Letters won't get us through that gate. I reckon we might as well pack up and go home.'

Mr Fox clawed at his hair. 'All the way back to London? We'd arrive in the middle of the night. How would we get all the boys back to their homes?'

'I'm pretty sure I could climb over that gate, sir,' said Hadley.

He sounded, thought Jonathan, like one of those young officers in old war movies – the brave but dim ones who volunteer for suicide missions. Still, thought Jonathan, Hadley was Captain of Games, and Head Boy as well so no doubt he had a position to keep up.

Mr Fox had no use for heroics either. 'I really don't see how that would improve the situation, Hadley. You'd be inside, we'd still be outside and the gate would still be locked.'

'I could go up to the house and see if there's anyone there, sir.'

'He's like the mug in horror movies,' whispered Timothy. 'There's always someone at the beginning who says, "Vampires? Superstitious nonsense. *I'll* walk home through the old dark churchyard . . . " And you know straight away what's going to happen to *him.*'

'If there was anyone in the house, Hadley,' Mr Fox was saying, 'they would presumably have come to the gate and let us in.'

'Then Mr Hughes is right, sir, we might as well pack up and go home.'

Mr Fox looked wildly from Hadley to Huw Hughes, feeling trapped. Somehow going or staying were both equally unappealing.

His dilemma was resolved by the sound of an ancient sports car which puttered up the lane behind them.

A tall, balding, bespectacled man leaped out, waving a bunch of keys. 'I say, I'm frightfully sorry.'

'Ah, Mr Davenport,' said Mr Fox frostily. 'There you are.'

'I had to go into town to pick up more supplies and the old bus broke down three times on the way back.'

Jonathan nudged Timothy. 'I'm not surprised, it looks as if it belongs in a motor museum.'

Mr Davenport's car was a huge green Bentley with big leather straps round the body – presumably to hold it together, thought Jonathan.

Mr Davenport was wrestling with the padlock and chains. 'Give us a hand somebody, will you?'

Hadley, keen as ever, ran to help. The rusty gates creaked open, and soon the coach was trundling up the gravel drive.

Another of Mr Davenport's keys unlocked the creaky front door, and he went inside. They saw the flare of a match, and soon a dim yellowish light revealed a huge oak-panelled hall.

'Gas lighting,' explained Mr Davenport proudly. 'Quite a curiosity really.'

Clutching their luggage the little party shuffled none too eagerly inside.

Mr Davenport turned to the two teachers. 'If you'd like to come with me, gentlemen, we'll see about getting organised.'

'Right, you lot,' said Mr Fox. 'Just wait here quietly till we get back. Hadley, you're in charge.'

The three adults disappeared further into the house, leaving an uneasy group of boys behind them. Jonathan couldn't help noticing that Briggsy, usually the biggest loud-mouth in the class, was the quietest and most uneasy-looking of them all.

Creeping up behind him, Jonathan said, 'Boo!' right in his ear.

Briggsy went white and jumped a foot in the air. 'Pack it up, Jonno, you could give someone a heart-attack.'

'All right, Dent, no clowning,' said Hadley nervously.

'Sorry,' said Jonathan. He turned to Timothy. 'It does look a bit sinister, doesn't it?'

119

Timmy gulped, trying to put a brave face on it. 'Oh, I don't know. Just your average everyday haunted house.'

They were standing at the foot of a huge staircase, which led upwards into pitch darkness. There was even the traditional suit of armour standing at its foot. Family portraits lined the oak-panelled walls of the hall. Between them were shields, crossed swords, and various antique weapons.

Two huge portraits hung to one side of the big staircase. One showed a thin, white-faced man in the dress of an eighteenth-century clergyman. He was holding a hymn-book and wearing a determinedly pious expression.

The other portrait showed a tough but cheerful-looking character in eighteenth-century riding dress. He carried a sporting gun and a brandy-flask, and there were gun-dogs at his feet.

For all their outward differences the two men were strangely alike, and somehow Jonathan felt sure they must be brothers.

For some reason, he found the two portraits strangely compelling. He was gazing at them in fascination when raised voices made him

aware that an argument had broken out.

Briggsy had recovered his nerve and was being his old obnoxious self. He was picking on Timothy.

'Haunted house!' he jeered. 'Ghosts! Trust a weed like you to believe in that rubbish!' He saw Jonathan watching him and broadened his attack. 'I suppose you believe in spooks as well.'

'I like to keep an open mind,' said Jonathan. 'Of course, to do that you have to have one to keep open.'

Briggsy clenched his fists. Then he unclenched them. He wasn't very bright, but he was bright enough to remember that all his previous attempts to thump Jonathan had ended in disaster.

'Well, I'm not scared,' he boasted. 'I'm going to take a look upstairs. Coming, Jonno – or are you too scared?'

Jonathan sighed. 'All right, if you insist.'

'Now just a minute,' said Hadley.

'Don't get your knickers in a twist, Hadders,' said Briggs. 'We'll just go to the top of the stairs.'

He set off up the big staircase, and Jonathan followed.

He remembered all Dave's warnings – but it was too late to think about that.

The first part of the journey was all right, they were still in the circle of light from the hall. But the top of the staircase was in deep shadow, and the passageway beyond in almost total darkness.

Hadley's voice came floating upwards. 'You

chaps all right? You'd better come down now.'

'All right, Briggsy,' whispered Jonathan as they reached the top of the stairs. 'You've proved your point. Let's go back down, Hadley's getting nervous.'

'You mean you are. I'm going to explore.'

Briggs took a few cautious steps along the pitch-black corridor – then stopped with a gasp of horror.

A billowing white shape had appeared in front of him. It had arms and legs and a blobby head and it was floating towards him moaning hideously.

'Spooks!' yelled Briggsy.

Whirling round he rushed past Jonathan, thundered down the staircase, across the hall and disappeared into the night.

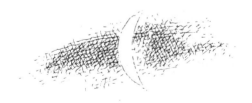

CHAPTER FOUR
Ghost Story

'As a matter of fact, the Old Manor *is* supposed to be haunted,' said Mr Davenport over supper. 'It all goes back to our family scandal – The Dark Deed of the Davenports. Now I've inherited I'm planning to write a book about it. I'm a historian, you know. While uncle was alive he always refused to give me access to the family papers – the library here is full of them. The whole story is very extensively documented, but it's been a family tradition to hush everything up. I think it's time it was brought to light.'

Despite his late arrival and his vague, scholarly manner, Mr Davenport seemed to have things surprisingly well organised. The cupboards in the enormous stone-flagged kitchen had been well stocked with food, and there was an old gas fridge and an even older cooking range, both still in working order.

The ever-efficient Hadley had soon organised a jobs rota and now they were tucking into sausages and chips washed down by mugs of steaming cocoa.

All this was after the panic caused by Briggsy's ghost-sighting had died down.

There had been utter pandemonium at the time.

Some of the more timid souls had joined Briggsy in a stampede from the house, while the rest had just milled about in confusion.

The intrepid Hadley had dashed up the stairs to save Jonathan from the spooks and found him standing quietly at the top of the stairs, looking thoughtfully along the corridor.

'What's happening?' Hadley had gasped. 'Where's the ghost?'

Jonathan had his own ideas about that, but all he'd said at the time was, 'I think it was just a flapping curtain on that window down there. Briggsy got himself all worked up and panicked when he saw something move.'

They'd gone back down the stairs, re-assured the others, and recaptured the fleeing Briggsy who was dashing down the lane apparently with the intention of running all the way back to London.

Poor old Briggs had had his leg pulled rotten after that, though not by Jonathan, and eventually the fuss had all died down.

Nevertheless, Jonathan was keenly interested in Mr Davenport's story. 'What is this Dark Deed of the Davenports, then?'

In a nice well-lit kitchen with hot food inside them, everyone was ready for a good ghost story and they all settled down to listen.

'Did anyone notice those two portraits in the hall?' Mr Davenport began.

'I did,' said Jonathan. 'Some sort of parson and a jolly-looking squire. They looked as if they might be brothers.'

'So they were,' said Mr Davenport. 'Back in the eighteenth century. The younger brother, the parson, was what you might call a high-flyer. Brilliant scholar, renowned for piety

and good works, everyone reckoned he'd finish up as a bishop. But he didn't quite make it for some reason, and eventually he came home and became parish priest of the local church.' Mr Davenport took a swig of cocoa. 'By this time his father had died and the elder brother was installed as the local squire. Now the elder brother was a very different type. Mad about hunting, shooting and fishing, rode to hounds every day in the season. Fond of the bottle, and even fonder of a tumble with the local girls.'

Briggs, now his old self again, said, 'Wor-hor-hey!'

'Briggs!' Mr Fox said sharply.

Mr Davenport coughed, and gave an embarrassed look at the two teachers.

'Sounds like a man after my own heart,' said Huw Hughes cheerfully.

Mr Fox said drily, 'I take it the two brothers did not get on well together?'

'They most certainly didn't! In fact, their quarrels were very soon the talk of the countryside. The priest was always reproving his brother about his wicked life, and the squire was always telling him to – well, get lost, I suppose.'

Mr Davenport paused dramatically. 'It all came to a head one dark and stormy night. The story goes that there was a particularly wild party going on at the hall. Unfortunately, the priest chose that night to visit his brother. He entered to find a scene of terrible debauchery.'

Briggsy started to say, 'Wor-hor- ' again.

'Shut up, Briggs, or I'll send you for a cold shower,' said Mr Fox. 'Forgive him, Mr Davenport, it's the hormones you know. Any hint of a mention of the opposite, er, gender, and he becomes positively rabid. Do go on.'

'Well, apparently the brothers had one last

128

terrible quarrel – which ended when the squire produced a pistol and shot his brother dead.'

The audience gave a satisfying gasp, and Mr Davenport went on, 'All the guests fled in horror, and the squire himself disappeared abroad soon afterwards.'

Timothy was goggle-eyed. 'What happened next?'

'The family tried to hush it all up. They said the priest died in a shooting accident and buried him with suspicious speed in the family chapel. But of course the story soon got about. The countryside was filled with rumours for years.'

'What happened to the squire?' asked Jonathan.

'He eventually came back to England and was promptly killed – in a duel probably. He's supposed to be buried in the grounds – in an unmarked grave.'

'Who haunts the Manor then?' asked Jonathan. 'The murdered priest or the wicked squire?'

'Well, both brothers have been sighted over the years. Mind, I've been living here for a couple of months now and I haven't seen any sign of them,' said Mr Davenport. 'And apparently there's the ghost of a little girl as well. So there you are then, you can't say we don't give good value. Not just one ghost, but three!'

'Do they just appear and disappear?' asked Timothy, 'or are they supposed to be dangerous?'

Mr Davenport looked uneasy. 'Well, there have been a few – accidents – over the years, mostly to children who climbed into the grounds to play. One was nearly killed. No local child has been near this place for years. So, be careful tomorrow when you're out and about.'

Mr Fox rose. 'And on that cheerful note we shall all go to bed – after the washing-up, of course. Your bedrooms are on the first and second floors – Mr Davenport will show you where they are. Breakfast will be at eight o'clock sharp. Be sure to consult with Hadley to see if you are on breakfast duty.'

Mr Fox paused. 'The gas lighting only covers the ground floor, so Hadley and the older boys will all be given candle-holders and candles. They will be responsible for seeing you don't make a bonfire of yourselves.'

When the washing-up was done, they all filed upstairs to bed.

Most of them were sleeping in one huge room converted into a dormitory. But there weren't quite enough beds in it, so a couple of boys were going to have to sleep in rooms by themselves. They drew lots and Jonathan and Timothy lost out. Timothy was nervous, but Jonathan was quite pleased.

Each was given his own candle, and off they went to their separate rooms.

Not long afterwards, Jonathan was lying in bed, which happened to be an enormous four-poster. He'd pulled back the bed-curtains – with them drawn it was like sleeping in a musty velvet tent.

He'd pulled back the window curtain too. Through the open window he could see the crescent moon against a background of black, wind-driven storm clouds.

On the little night-stand beside his bed, his stub of candle was burning low.

Suddenly it guttered and went out.

Jonathan didn't move. He just lay there, waiting.

Soon his window curtain began to move.

A billowing white shape appeared.

It had a blobby head and stubby arms and legs.

It moved towards him making weird noises. 'Woo-oo-oo,' it moaned. 'Woo-oo-oo!'

Jonathan yawned. 'Come off it, Dave. I've seen your spook act before. It wasn't all that convincing the first time!'

CHAPTER FIVE
The Buried Past

Dave threw aside the sheet and perched on the end of the bed, grinning cheekily. 'It was good enough for old Briggsy, wasn't it?'

'Briggsy's a moron,' said Jonathan impatiently. 'Look, Dave, what do you think you're up to, carrying on like this. I thought you promised not to make life difficult for me any more.'

Dave's grin faded. 'Believe me, mate, I am not just mucking about. I'm trying to save you from some horrible fate. I thought if I gave Briggsy a good scare you might all change your minds and go home after all.'

'But why are you so keen for us to go? Is

this place really haunted – apart from you, I mean?'

'Haunted? I'll say it's haunted! I reckon there are at least three Earthbound spirits.'

'Mr Davenport said there were three ghosts,' said Jonathan. He gave Dave a potted version of the story Davenport had told them over supper.

Dave listened thoughtfully. 'Well, that could account for it, I suppose.'

'Have you managed to communicate at all?'

Dave shook his head. 'Not really, we're not on the same wavelength you might say. You see, Earthbound spirits are all wrapped up in whatever it is that's keeping them Earthbound. I'm different. I come back to Earth because I want to, with them, it's usually something pretty fierce, sort of obsessing them. Hatred, revenge . . . or maybe a need for justice, wanting the truth to come out . . . Like that Spitfire Pilot we ran into at your Great-Aunt's house.'

'So what is it with this lot?'

'It's all mixed up,' said Dave. 'One of them, the worst, is more or less pure evil. All I pick up off him is like a rage to hurt or destroy – as if he wanted revenge on the whole human race. The other one's just angry and baffled, as if there's something he wants to do and can't . . . '

'And the third spirit?'

'I think that must be the little girl. It just feels sort of sad and lost . . . '

Jonathan sat up in bed, thinking hard. The trouble with this sort of problem was, there was no-one you could share it with. He certainly couldn't go to Foxy or Huw Hughes.

'Dave, do you *really* think we're in danger? Could one of these spirits actually hurt someone? I mean, what could they do – materialise and give someone a nasty fright, I suppose, but what else?'

'You just don't understand,' said Dave despairingly. 'There's so much bottled-up psychic energy in this place it's like a volcano. Someone could be driven mad, or even killed. They could lose their soul.'

'Can't you get in touch with them, find out what they want? Maybe we could help, like we did with the Spitfire Pilot.'

'I can try,' said Dave dubiously. 'But it's dangerous for me as well, you know.'

'Why, what could they do to you? I mean, you're a . . . ' Jonathan broke off, not sure how to put what he wanted to say.

'A ghost already?' said Dave. 'Maybe I am, but that doesn't mean I've got nothing to lose. If I start messing about with spirits as powerful as these, I could get wiped out on the spiritual plane.'

'What does that mean?'

'It could mean I didn't exist at all – in your world or in the next.'

Jonathan looked helplessly at him. 'So what do we do?'

'Lay low – and whatever you do, don't go out of your room till daylight. I'll sort of watch over things as best I can.'

'Is there anything I can do to help?'

'I'm afraid not,' said Dave grimly. 'This is down to me. A ghost's gotta do what a ghost's gotta do . . . Wish me luck!'

And with that he faded away.

Jonathan lay back on his pillows, wondering if he would ever get to sleep. The affairs of the spirit world seemed confused and complicated, he thought. He'd got used to Dave, but it was strange to think that there

were ghosts even Dave was frightened of . . .
The pillows were soft and the room was dark
and Jonathan had had a tiring day. Despite
all his worries he found himself drifting off to
sleep.

The trouble with going to sleep is that
you're liable to dream . . .

*Jonathan was drifting slowly on a sea of
darkness. It was a sensation he'd felt before,
and somehow he knew that he wasn't just
asleep, he was out of his body, drifting on
what Dave would have called the spiritual
plane.*

*There was a girl, somewhere ahead of him
in the distance. She was young and thin and
frightened-looking, wearing an old-fashioned
nightgown. She was calling him, she wanted
him to go with her . . . But Jonathan still had
Dave's warnings in his head and he wasn't
sure . . .*

*All at once there was a man with the girl – a
tough-looking man in riding dress with a
smoking pistol in his hand. It was the squire,
the one who'd murdered his brother . . .*

He wanted Jonathan to go with him as well.

There was something he had to show him, something vitally important.

Jonathan struggled to resist. The man was a murderer, he couldn't be trusted . . .

Suddenly there was a black-clad white-faced figure in the way. It was the murdered priest. He seemed to be sending off waves of cold anger, telling Jonathan the other spirits were evil, that he mustn't listen to them . . .

Still the squire and the girl beckoned to him, the squire waving his smoking pistol.

It was strange how real it all seemed, thought Jonathan. Even though he knew it was only a dream he could actually *smell* the smoke from the squire's pistol.

Suddenly Jonathan realised he was awake.

He was awake – but he could still smell smoke.

Without even thinking about Dave's warning, Jonathan leaped out of bed and dashed out of his room.

There was a haze of smoke in the corridor outside and a nearby flickering of flames.

Smoke and light were both coming from the next room – Timothy's room.

Jonathan ran to the doorway.

Timothy lay on his bed, asleep as if in a trance.

The curtains near his bed were all ablaze.

Jonathan started to go to him – and suddenly the white-faced priest was in the doorway, barring his way.

Whatever warning the spirit was trying to give, Jonathan didn't have time for it.

He dashed straight *through* the apparition, and knocked Timothy from the bed, falling to the floor on top of him.

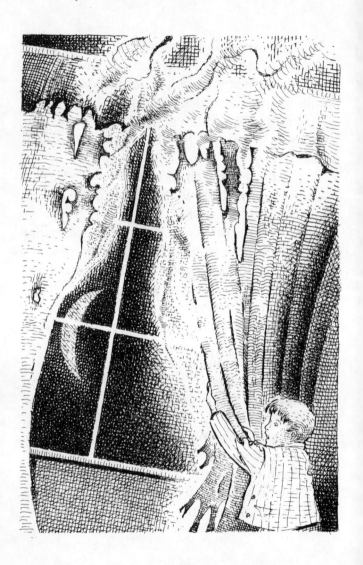

Timothy came awake with a yell of alarm, clutching wildly at him.

'Wake up, Timmy, there's a fire,' shouted Jonathan. 'Go and give the alarm.'

Timothy ran into the corridor shouting, 'Fire! Fire! Fire!'

Jonathan dragged down the blazing curtains and tried to smother them with the blankets from the bed.

Suddenly the room was full of people helping him, and soon the flames were beaten down.

Hadley came rushing in with a bucket of water which he hurled across the bed, not realising that Huw Hughes was stamping out flames on the other side.

Unfortunately, Huw Hughes stood up just as Hadley let fly with the contents of the bucket . . .

For a moment Huw Hughes just stood there, dripping quietly into the charred carpet. Then he said quietly, 'Thank you Hadley, most refreshing.'

Hadley gulped and hurried away.

Gradually everyone calmed down and Jonathan told Mr Fox what had happened.

He decided it was best to keep it simple, so he just said he'd been woken by the smell of smoke and got up to find Timmy's curtains on fire. 'I woke Timothy up and sent him to give the alarm, and did my best to smother the flames.'

'You did very well,' said Mr Fox. 'Very well indeed.' He sighed wearily. 'Well, I suppose if boys have to be given candles at least one of them is bound to be careless – and one is all it takes.' He looked down at Timothy. 'I must say I'm surprised it was you though, I thought you were such a sensible boy.'

Timothy was white-faced and shaken. 'But it wasn't, sir, I mean I didn't. I put the candle out very carefully before I went to sleep. I remember doing it.'

Timothy was very distressed and Mr Fox patted him awkwardly on the back. 'I'm sure you think you did.' He looked round the smoke-blackened room. 'However, the evidence does seem to suggest you were mistaken! Come on, we must find you somewhere else to sleep. I trust the school insurance will pay for the damage.'

Still protesting, Timmy was led away and

everyone started drifting back to their own beds.

When he got back to his room, Jonathan wasn't surprised to find Dave waiting for him.

'See?' said Dave simply. 'What did I tell you?'

Wearily Jonathan climbed back into bed. 'I suppose it could have been an accident . . .'

'Don't you believe it. There was something very sinister going on tonight. I tried to warn you, but there was no way I could overcome the evil force. It was just too powerful for me.'

'It's certainly not like Timmy to be careless,' said Jonathan thoughtfully. 'He's one of life's worriers, checks everything ten times over. You think it was one of the Earthbound spirits set fire to the curtains. Would they be able to?'

Dave nodded. 'Dead easy! It doesn't take much psychic energy to light a candle, I could do it myself. Not that I would, of course. I tell you, mate, that was no accident. One of those spirits is a killer – and it wants fresh blood!'

Jonathan had been thinking hard about what had happened – and he'd come up with a very worrying theory. 'Old Davenport was saying something about accidents,' he said. 'Accidents to ids playing in the grounds. He said no local child has been near this place for years. Do you reckon this evil spirit of yours hates children – children particularly, I mean, more than anyone else?'

Dave shrugged. 'Could do, I suppose . . . What are you getting at?'

Jonathan went on with his theory. 'Let's say I'm right, and for some reason this particular ghost hates kids. Well, there haven't been any children living here for years, and according to you, it can't go out and hunt for them . . . '

Dave nodded. 'The thing about Earthbound spirits is, they're usually tied pretty strictly to one place. They can't go wandering round the country the way I do.'

'It'd just have to lie in wait then, wouldn't it?' said Jonathan slowly. 'Maybe pounce on some village kid who was daft enough to climb into the grounds. And when they stopped coming, it'd just get hungrier and hungrier . . . And then we turn up. A whole busload of lambs, wandering into the lion's den. Victims all over the place . . . it can pick and choose!'

'That's right, mate – and you know who it's liable to pick next, don't you? You!'

'Me?' said Jonathan uneasily. 'Why me?'

'Spoiled its fun, didn't you? It was all set to turn young Timmy to a crisp and you interfered. It's not going to like that . . . '

Jonathan drew a deep breath. 'So what do I do?'

'Stay awake,' said Dave simply. 'As much as you can, anyway. I'll do my best to look after you, but this thing's a lot more powerful than I am . . . You stay here, and I'll scout around, see if it's still hanging about. And, remember, don't go to sleep!'

Before Jonathan could say anything, Dave just faded away.

Jonathan piled his pillows up high, re-lit his candle, and dug out a biology textbook from his knapsack. 'A good dose of scientific fact,' he thought, 'that's what I need.'

He did his best to stay awake.

But when you're young and you've had a tiring and exciting day, staying awake is one of the hardest things to do.

Even if going to sleep could cost you your life.

The candle flame waved and flickered and the words of the textbook blurred before his eyes . . .

Jonathan thought about getting up, walking round the room. But even as he was thinking about it, his head nodded and he was dreaming . . .

He dreamed he was floating away on a warm dark sea . . .

He didn't see the dark figure that materialised in the corner of the room, eyes gleaming with hate.

It raised its hand. The heavy old-fashioned bedspread rose in the air, hovered, and wrapped itself round Jonathan's head and shoulders. Still drifting in a warm soft darkness, Jonathan suddenly became aware that the dark sea had become solid. It was suffocating him, choking him. The worst thing about it was that he couldn't move . . .

He fought for breath, a roaring in his head. He felt himself sinking . . .

A sudden sharp pain in his ankle jolted him awake.

Jonathan panicked, wrestling with the bedspread, struggling to get free. He realised that someone was helping, pulling the bedspread from his face . . .

Panting, Jonathan struggled clear, and immediately the bedspread dropped to the ground, just a harmless piece of cloth.

Dave was looking at him in concern. 'You all right, mate?'

'I think so . . . What happened?'

'It tricked me,' said Dave bitterly. 'Sort of lured me away. Finally I realised, shot back here – and found the bedspread attacking you like a boa-constrictor.'

'Why's my ankle so sore?'

'Well, you were just lying there. I had to give you a kick on the ankle to wake you up!'

'Thanks a lot!' said Jonathan. Then he looked serious. 'I mean it, Dave, thanks. You saved my life.'

Dave looked embarrassed. 'Shouldn't have left you, should I?'

'What do we do now?'

'Sit it out till morning. I'll see you don't nod off. Don't worry, I'm a ghost, I don't need sleep.'

Dave and Jonathan sat chatting through the hours of darkness, and every time Jonathan's head nodded, Dave's bony elbow jolted him awake.

Finally Dave looked out of the window. A few pale streaks were appearing in the sky and the birds were starting to kick up a racket. 'It's nearly dawn now. Even the worst evil spirit's powers aren't so strong when the day's beginning. I reckon you can risk a few hours' kip . . .'

CHAPTER SIX
Ghostly Attack

It took a long time for Jonathan to get off to sleep, even though he was aware of Dave sitting on the end of the bed watching over him.

He didn't really drop off until well after dawn, and even then his sleep was fitful and uneasy.

He was awakened by someone shaking him. 'Jonathan! Wake up! Wake up!'

He opened his eyes to find Timmy standing over him. 'Come on Jonathan, wake up, we've overslept. We'll be late for breakfast.'

Jonathan staggered out of bed and after a quick wash and dress he and Timothy hurried downstairs.

As they crossed the hall, Timothy came to a sudden halt before the two big portraits. 'That picture, it was in my dream. I dreamed he was there in my room. He was holding a candle high above his head.'

'Who – the wicked squire?'

'No, no, the other one – the murdered priest. Now, why should I dream that?'

Jonathan tried to reassure him. 'Why shouldn't you? You saw the portrait last night, then Mr Davenport told us the story. I expect it all got mixed up in your mind. Dreams are often like that, mix-ups of what's been going on. Some people think dreams are just the mind clearing its memory banks.'

Timothy said seriously, 'I didn't leave that candle burning last night, you know. I really didn't. You know what a fuss-pot I am. I was terrified of starting a fire the minute I got the candle and I checked it was really out at least a dozen times.'

'I believe you, Timmy,' said Jonathan gently. 'I really do.'

'Then how did the fire start?'

'Beats me,' said Jonathan. But his mind was filled with the picture of Timothy and the blazing curtains.

Those curtains had been burning from the top. There was no way a knocked-over candle could have come anywhere near the place where the fire had begun . . .

The fire had been started deliberately. But who would have done it? Surely the obvious candidate was the wicked squire. But why had Timothy dreamed about the priest?

Maybe the priest had tried to stop it, just as he'd warned Jonathan away from the fire last night. Timothy had seen him and got muddled . . .

Jonathan sighed. 'Never mind, Timmy, just try and forget about it. Let's go in for some breakfast.'

First thing on the agenda after breakfast was Applied Botany. This boiled down to a wander round the Old Manor House's incredibly large and overgrown garden, looking vaguely for any interesting plants.

'There's a pond and a little stream right down the bottom of the garden,' said Mr Davenport. 'Watch out for the pond though, it's surprisingly deep. In fact the locals say it's bottomless.'

It was a hot sunny morning and they were all bursting to get outside. Before long everyone was happily pottering along the banks of the stream or studying the edge of the pond, which was rich in plant life.

Foxy and Huw Hughes supervised from beneath the shade of a convenient oak tree.

There was frogspawn in the pond and Robbie Peters, one of the younger boys, had come armed with a jam-jar and a fishing net. Jonathan watched as he leaned over the pond, reaching out for a big clump of frogspawn.

He saw Hadley come up behind Peters, and assumed he was going to offer to help, making use of his longer reach.

Then he saw the expression on Hadley's face. It was cold and cruel. In fact it didn't look like Hadley at all.

Hadley looked like someone else – someone different and yet familiar. To Jonathan's astonishment, this strange Hadley leaned forwards and deliberately shoved Peters into the pond.

Jonathan reacted without thinking.

He dived in, grabbed the frantically struggling Peters and shoved him towards the bank, where willing hands heaved them both out, dripping with weed.

Mr Fox and Huw Hughes came hurrying up.

Mr Fox looked at Jonathan. 'Well done! We'll have to put you in for the Lifesaving Medal. Now, you'd both better get back to the house and get into something dry.'

On the way Jonathan squelched over to Hadley. Somehow he just had to convince him he wasn't to blame. Hadley was staring fixedly into the pond. 'You mustn't blame yourself, Hadley, you did your best.'

Hadley stared wildly at him. 'My best – but I . . .'

'Peters slipped, and you tried to grab him but missed,' said Jonathan firmly. 'Isn't that right, Robbie?'

Little Peters couldn't really remember what had happened and he certainly wasn't going to argue with his heroic rescuer. 'Yes, that's right. I felt you trying to grab me as I slipped.'

Hadley's face cleared. 'Yes, that's right. I'd better keep the others away from the edge of the pond.'

Hadley hurried off, and Peters and Jonathan made their way back to the house for some dry clothes.

Jonathan had just finished changing in his room when Dave appeared. 'Something's happened, I can feel it.'

Jonathan told him about Hadley's strange behaviour.

'He was taken over,' said Dave at once. 'Possessed!'

'Yes, but why? What does this spirit want?'

'Death,' said Dave slowly. 'I can feel it. Somehow it was cheated of a death in the past and it wants to claim one now. It won't rest until it's killed someone.'

'I think you're right. You know what keeps worrying me, Dave? Apart from having a homicidal spook on the loose, that is?'

'What?'

'The story's all wrong.'

'What story?'

'The one Davenport told us, the Daven-ports' Dark Deed. It doesn't fit what's been happening – and it doesn't fit what you found out about these Earthbound spirits – or what I feel about them either.'

'How do you mean?'

'Well, all that stuff about one of them being

angry and baffled. The way I felt the girl and the squire wanted to tell me something . . . It just doesn't fit.'

'Fit what?'

Jonathan struggled to explain. 'Look, the story Davenport told us is too straight-forward, too cut and dried. Bad brother murders good brother, comes to a bad end. End of story. There's no mystery, no secret, nothing to explain what's been going on or why one of the spirits turned so murderous. Unless . . . '

'Unless what?'

'Unless the story's all wrong . . . ' Jonathan shook his head. 'But it can't be, Davenport said it was all confirmed in family records and local histories.' Jonathan got up and started pacing about the room. 'So we've got to accept that the squire did kill his brother – but maybe the story gets the reasons all wrong. Maybe the killing was – justified in some way.'

'Pretty hard to justify killing your own brother, especially when he's a priest.'

'I know,' said Jonathan gloomily. 'And where does the little girl fit in? I'm just going round in circles. The funny thing is, when Timothy's curtains were on fire I saw the priest trying to *stop* me getting to him. And Timothy dreamed he saw the *priest* holding the candle.' Jonathan came to a sudden halt in the centre of the room. 'And when Hadley was shoving poor old Peters in the pond, he looked just like the priest in the portrait!' He looked excitedly at Dave. 'I can't prove it, but I'm convinced of it. Somehow or other it's the priest who's the villain of the piece, and the priest's ghost is the murderous one . . .'

Suddenly Dave leaped from the bed and shoved Jonathan clear across the room – just as the heavy glass chandelier crashed down on the spot where he'd just been standing.

Jonathan leaned gasping against the wall. 'Thanks, Dave.' He looked at the ruins of the chandelier. 'You know, something tells me we're on the right track!'

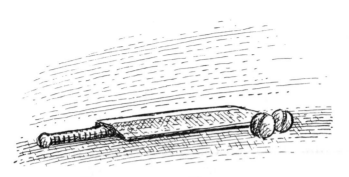

CHAPTER SEVEN

Dangerous Quest

Mr Davenport was very nice about the chandelier. He said it was an old house and bits were dropping off all the time.

As the afternoon wore on the heat became almost unbearable. Nobody really wanted to do anything but lie down in the shade and rest.

Mr Fox wasn't having that.

He organised a game of cricket. He was the captain of one side, and Huw Hughes captained the other.

Foxy won the toss, and put himself in to bat.

A nervous Timothy bowled him the first

ball, and Mr Fox sent it streaking to the boundary for four.

He hit the next ball for a six . . .

Jonathan was in Huw Hughes's team and as he stood perspiring in the outfield, waiting for his turn to bowl, Dave popped up beside him. 'Enjoying yourself ?'

Jonathan mopped his forehead. 'Not really!'

Dave gave an elaborate yawn. 'Old Foxy looks set to stay there all day. I'd offer you a bit of help, but I know you don't like me to interfere . . . '

'I think this is a special case.'

Jonathan went over to Huw Hughes who was gloomily watching the slaughter. 'Give us a chance at bowling, sir.'

'You must be mad, boy, wanting to expend energy on a day like this. Still, suit yourself.'

Next over, Huw Hughes put Jonathan on to bowl.

Jonathan faced up to the mighty Foxy.

He bowled him a slow googly.

Mr Fox smiled evilly, stepped confidently forward, and raised his bat. Somehow the ball seemed to hover for a moment. Then it

shot between his legs and took out his middle
stump.

With an outraged glare Foxy stalked from
the field.

It was Hadley's turn to face the bowling
and Jonathan sent him a sizzling fast one.

Hadley stepped confidently to meet it – but
he stumbled over some invisible obstacle and
the ball shattered his wicket.

Jonathan bowled out the next batsman too
– and the next and the next . . .

When Foxy's team were all out, Jonathan and Huw Hughes went in to open for their side.

'I warn you, I'm a terrible cricketer,' rumbled Huw Hughes.

'Just leave it all to me, sir. Keep the batting my end and we'll be okay.'

Hadley bowled the first ball, a slow twister, which seemed to check at the last minute and hover invitingly in front of Jonathan's bat.

Jonathan hit it for six.

He hit the next ball for a six and most of the rest of the over as well, varying it with the occasional four.

He was well on the way to beating Foxy's fifty when it happened. Hadley ran up to bowl his next ball. He was a fairly tricky slow bowler, but Jonathan was confident he could handle him – especially with a little help from Dave.

But suddenly Hadley wasn't a slow bowler any more. He took a long run and pounded up to the crease, his face a mask of hatred – just the way it had looked when he tried to push Peters in the pond.

The ball shot from his hand with

superhuman force – straight for Jonathan's head.

Jonathan just managed to get his bat up in time.

The force of the ball splintered the bat and the deflected ball grazed Jonathan's forehead.

For a moment the whole field of players stood frozen in astonishment.

'Are you all right?' called Foxy.

Jonathan nodded dumbly.

Hadley seemed to be dazed . . .

There was a sudden tremendous thunderclap, a flash of sheet lightning and suddenly the rain came pouring down.

'Game over,' shouted Foxy. 'We'll call it a draw, rain stopped play!'

As he ran back to the house, Jonathan wasn't thinking about cricket.

He knew he'd had another lucky escape from the power of the malignant spirit.

It seemed determined to kill somebody. And at the moment it seemed determined to kill him.

After supper Jonathan had a long talk with Mr Davenport about the family scandal. Pleased by his interest Mr Davenport took him to the study and showed him the family papers. They told the full story of the murder of the priest and the squire's flight and subsequent death.

The story was confirmed in every detail – there was even a display case with relics of the brothers, the priest's cross and hymnbook, and the squire's riding crop and brandy-flask and pistol.

When Mr Davenport was searching for a copy of the local history, Jonathan on a sudden impulse slipped the squire's gun and the priest's cross from the display case into his pocket.

Night fell as it always must, and it was time for bed.

Foxy and Huw Hughes carried out a candle patrol, checking that every candle was well and truly out.

Once they'd left Jonathan's room, Dave appeared on the end of Jonathan's bed. 'Well, now what?'

'I'm going to sleep – and if the squire turns up again, I'm going to go with him.'

'Suppose you're wrong?' said Dave. 'Suppose he is an evil spirit after all? I won't let you do it, it's far too dangerous.'

'It's too dangerous not to. You said yourself – it, whoever or whatever it is, wants a death. It's attacked three of us now – Timothy, little Peters and now me. No adults, you notice. I think my idea was right – it wants to kill a child. If I don't stop it now it's bound to get one of us eventually – most likely me, since it knows I'm on to it.'

'All right,' said Dave wearily. 'If you must, you must. I'll give you what help I can, but I can't promise too much.'

Jonathan lay back on his pillows and waited for sleep.

He fell into it almost at once, like dropping into a black pit.

Suddenly he felt he was floating.

A figure appeared before him. It was the squire, pistol in hand. He beckoned, and Jonathan followed.

All at once they were tramping through the garden, the storm howling over their heads. Not they, Jonathan realised suddenly. Somehow he wasn't with the squire any more, he was the squire, seeing events through his eyes, understanding them through his brain.

Now it was a night two hundred years ago, and he was tramping through the rain-sodden garden towards the family chapel, dreading what he would find.

He heard the sound of chanting as he drew nearer.

It seemed to be rising to a crescendo.

He reached the wooden door of the chapel and hurled it open.

A service was taking place – but no ordinary service.

It was a ceremony of evil – of devil worship. Lying on the altar was a young girl, and *standing over her was a scarlet-robed figure in a goat-mask, a knife raised high.*

As the knife swept down the squire drew the pistol from his pocket and fired – one bullet through the heart.

The robed figure fell across the body of its intended victim.

Ignoring the shrieking figures rushing past him and out into the night he strode over to the altar and snatched the mask from the high priest.

His brother's dead face stared up at him.

He lifted the fainting child from the altar and carried her back towards the house.

Suddenly Jonathan was himself again, floating once more in limbo. This time it was the girl who appeared before him, beckoning.

Once again Jonathan followed.

He knew now that she was the girl on the altar, the one the squire had saved at the cost of his brother's life.

She took him to the hall and showed him a secret panel in the wall, between the portraits of the two brothers. Inside was a sealed earthenware jar.

She raised her hand in farewell and disappeared.

Suddenly Jonathan realised he was awake – and back in his bed. He knew the truth now, knew what he must do.

With a sigh of relief Jonathan opened his eyes.

The priest was standing over him, knife in hand . . .

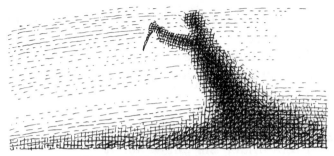

CHAPTER EIGHT

The Final Truth

For a moment the white face glared down at him, eyes blazing with hate.

Then the knife swept down.

Suddenly Dave appeared from nowhere, knocking aside the descending arm.

For a moment the two grappled, but the years of hate had given the priest more stored-up psychic energy than Dave could muster.

Dave was flung aside with ease and the knife arm rose again . . .

But Dave's intervention had given Jonathan the time he needed.

From under his pillow he took the silver

cross that had belonged to the priest and held it up.

For a moment the symbol of the religion he had dishonoured seemed to freeze the priest where he stood.

But only for a moment.

Slowly, the knife arm rose again.

From under the pillow Jonathan snatched the squire's pistol and trained it on the priest's heart.

The pistol was empty of course.

But in the spirit world of the ghostly priest, the pistol roared as it had two hundred years ago, and he felt the shock of the bullet in his heart.

The second, symbolic death seemed to

release him from his long years of hate-filled bondage to Earth.

The ghostly body shattered and dispersed and the knife clattered to the floor and vanished.

Jonathan fell back on his pillow with a gasp of relief and looked up at Dave. 'I think we did it,' he said. 'It's over.'

Next day, Jonathan recovered the sealed jar from the secret panel beneath the portraits. It proved to contain a thick wodge of papers sealed in a sort of oilskin parcel. Jonathan handed them over to Mr Davenport who disappeared into the study with them and wasn't seen again till dinner-time.

When supper was over Mr Davenport said, 'When you first came here I told you all the story of our family legend. I'm afraid most of it was lies. Now I'm going to tell you the story again – this time it will be the truth.'

Mr Davenport said the first part of the legend had been true enough. Failing in his ambitions, the talented young priest came home, and took up an appointment in his local church.

'Bitterly disappointed by the failure of his ambitions he sought power by other means. If he could not be God's Bishop, he would be the devil's. He became a Satanist, and recruited other local notables to his evil cult.

'His brother the squire was horrified when he heard the rumours about what was going on. At first he refused to believe it.

'Then, one night, he came to the family chapel and found an evil ceremony in progress and a child about to be sacrificed. To save the child he killed his brother, and to save the family name he fled abroad. But the dead priest had friends in high places. To save his reputation and their own, they slandered the missing squire and spread a story that turned truth on its head. When the squire returned to England to clear his name, they murdered him, and buried him on his estate in an unmarked grave.' Mr Davenport tapped the pile of papers. 'The true story and the location of the grave are both in these papers, written by the girl the squire saved from sacrifice. She was afraid to tell the truth at the time, the squire's enemies were too powerful. But luckily she left this record

behind her – and, quite by chance I understand, Jonathan found it.'

Mr Davenport beamed round the table. 'I shall have my ancestor the squire re-buried in the family chapel, and I shall write a book that will clear his name!'

Everyone cheered, and then they all went up to bed.

'What I want now is a nice night's unhaunted

sleep,' said Jonathan as he climbed under the covers.

Dave looked indignant. 'Well, there's a nice thing to say.'

'Oh, I don't mean you,' said Jonathan sleepily. 'You're what you could call the school spirit! I'm used to you . . .'

Jonathan drifted off to sleep and Dave wandered round the house filled with sleeping kids.

'School spirit indeed,' thought Dave. 'Well, if I'm the school ghost, I'm entitled to do a bit of haunting.'

He found his white sheet and floated up and down the dark corridors.

'Woo-oo-ooo,' he wailed. 'Woo-oo-oo!'

But nobody took any notice.

They were all fast asleep.

Jonathan and
the Superstar

CHAPTER ONE

New Boy

'Storm at sea, boyo? Storm at sea? Looks more like a ripple on a duck pond to me! Looks like a bucket of cold cat-sick!' Huw Hughes stared scornfully at Jonathan's painting and waved his arms like a wild Welsh windmill. 'Let's have a bit of excitement, a bit of colour . . .'

Giving Jonathan's ear a painful tweak, he strode away.

It was a double art period, and everyone was beavering away, head down, deep in the throes of artistic creation.

'Art can't be taught, boyos,' Huw Hughes boomed at the beginning of the lesson. 'You can only learn by doing! Paint me . . . Paint me . . .' He looked out of the window for inspiration, and saw the wind tossing the leaves of the trees outside the classroom. 'Paint me – a storm at sea!'

He retreated to his private corner and got on with a painting of his own.

At heart Huw Hughes was more of an artist than an art teacher. Any day now he was going to knock spots off Van Gogh and all the lot of them.

A cheerful voice whispered in Jonathan's ear. 'Wants a bit of excitement does he? A bit of colour? I'll give him excitement! I'll give him colour!'

There didn't seem to be a boy attached to the voice – but Jonathan knew all too well who it was.

A pot of paint rose slowly from a shelf and hovered in the air, just over Huw Hughes's head.

'Dave, no . . .' whispered Jonathan, but it was already too late. The hovering paint pot tilted and slowly, very slowly, paint dripped onto Huw Hughes's left ear.

He was so absorbed he didn't notice at

first. Slowly he put a hand up to his head, took it away, and stared at it. His hand was wet – and green.

With a roar of anger he jumped back, banging into the wall behind him. Another pot of paint tipped over on the shelf above, dripping paint onto his right ear.

Huw Hughes put up his right hand, brought it away and looked thoughtfully at it.

This time the hand was red.

He just stood there for a moment, one green hand, one red hand, one red ear, one green ear.

A single blob of paint dropped from the shelf above, landing precisely on the end of his nose. It was bright yellow.

A boy at the back yelled, 'It's a traffic light!' and a roar of laughter shook the class.

Huw Hughes stood quite still until the laughter died down. Then he turned and stalked into the glassed-off corner cubbyhole.

'That's a good one, traffic light,' said a familiar voice. Lucky I chose those colours.'

Jonathan turned. Leaning against the wall beside him was a cheeky-looking boy of about his own age. But this boy wore baggy grey flannel shorts held up by a cricket belt with an S-shaped snake clasp, and a short-sleeved V-necked pullover over an open-necked shirt. His hair was cropped short in a 'Forties-style' short back and sides – otherwise known as a fourpenny all-off. It was Jonathan's best friend, Dave.

Dave was invisible when he wanted to

be, and even when he *was* visible, no-one could see him but Jonathan.

Dave was a ghost.

It had all started when Jonathan's family moved into the house where Dave's family had lived during the war.

Dave hadn't actually survived the war, he was killed when a doodlebug, one of Hitler's flying bombs, crashed into his attic bedroom. Dave had been haunting his old house ever since, bored and lonely and looking for a friend. At last he'd found one – Jonathan.

But it wasn't always easy, having a ghost for a friend. Like now, for instance.

'You've dropped me right in it now, haven't you,' said Jonathan angrily.

Dave looked innocent. 'Why? Nothing to do with you was it – you were nowhere near.'

'Look, Dave, how many times have I got to tell you? Whenever you pull one of these daft tricks people start looking at me!'

'Shouldn't have had a go at your painting, should he?' muttered Dave sulkily. 'Mind you, it could do with livening up a bit.' Suddenly Dave vanished. Tubes of paint started squirting colours onto Jonathan's palette. His brush leaped in the air all by itself and began slashing at the canvas.

'Pack it in,' hissed Jonathan, moving to screen all this frantic activity from the others.

Huw Hughes came out of his cubicle, paint-free and smelling strongly of turpentine.

He made straight for Jonathan. 'Now see here, boyo . . .'

He broke off as he caught sight of Jonathan's painting. The once-murky picture now showed swirling mountains of blue-green seas, broken up with turbulent white-capped waves. Art had been one of Dave's best subjects.

'I've, er, touched it up a bit,' said Jonathan hopefully. Huw Hughes stared hard at the painting, and even harder at Jonathan. 'They knew how to deal with witches and warlocks in the old days. Burned at the stake they were. I think I'll ask the Head if I can put up a stake in the playground.'

Before Huw Hughes could say any more Jonathan was saved by the end-of-lesson bell.

His friend Timothy, a very small boy with very big glasses, came up to him. 'Weird, that business about the paint . . .'

'I expect there's some perfectly natural explanation.'

'Oh, absolutely,' said Timmy. 'Vibrations from a passing lorry, paint pots tipped over on the shelf, old Huw standing underneath . . .

Funny the way he copped it, just after he'd been having a go at you over your painting.'

'Look, it was just coincidence, all right?'

'Don't get mad,' said Timmy hurriedly, backing away. 'Funny things happen to people you get mad at . . .'

'Great,' thought Jonathan as they headed for the next lesson. 'Now even Timmy thinks I've got evil powers!'

Dave just didn't seem to realise how much trouble he caused.

They had Mr Fox their form master for maths after the break. When they went into the classroom they saw there was someone with him, a tall, smartly dressed boy with neatly-brushed fair hair. 'We have a newcomer to the class,' announced Mr Fox. 'This is Jason Smythe. It will not have escaped the brighter ones that Jason is somewhat older than the rest of you. His education has been interrupted by frequent changes of school as his father works abroad.'

Foxy waved a hand around the class. 'I won't attempt to introduce all this motley crew, Jason, you'll soon get to know them all too well. There's a place for you at that table over there.'

Jason sat looking politely attentive throughout the lesson, and even put his hand up to answer one of Foxy's quick-fire mental maths questions towards the end. He even got it right.

Next lesson was French, and Jason did pretty well in that too. Mr Lemont the French teacher complimented him on his accent. Jason explained modestly that he'd gone to school in Paris for a while. 'I couldn't help picking up a *bit* of French . . .'

Although Jonathan was actually a bit on the shy side, he decided to go and introduce himself to Jason at lunchtime. His own parents had only recently moved to the area and he'd been a newcomer to the school himself not so long ago. He felt sure that Jason must be feeling a bit lost on his first day.

His plan was delayed when Mr Lemont nabbed him to take a note to the Head at the end of the lesson.

By the time Jonathan reached the dining

hall, Jason was already sitting down to lunch. Far from appearing lost or lonely, he was chatting away to an attentive audience. 'Paris was fun, and so was Rome,' he was saying. 'But I really think I liked New York the best.' He looked up and saw Jonathan. 'Come over and join us,' he called – just as if Jonathan was the new boy!

'Thanks a lot,' said Jonathan dryly.

Timmy squeezed up to make room for him and he sat down opposite Jason, who went on talking about his travels.

It seemed his father was an architect whose firm built hotels and office blocks all round the world. 'He stays with the job right from first plans till everything's finished,' Jason explained. 'So we end up living abroad for six months or a year at a time. Trouble is, the next job's in the Near East, and Dad put his foot down. Said he didn't want me ending up as a hostage!'

Jason went on chatting away about his travels.

Jonathan went on listening and quietly eating his hamburger and chips, wishing his own life had been half as interesting.

A voice in Jonathan's ear whispered, 'Goes on a bit, doesn't he?' Dave didn't seem to be too impressed.

Jason went on with his story – he was back in New York by now. Then, suddenly – 'Aaahhh!'

A loud yawn echoed across the table.

It came from right behind Jonathan – and sounded, of course, as if it came *from* him.

Jason looked up, but Jonathan was innocently munching chips. Jason went on with his story. 'So we went to this really terrific disco just off Broadway –'

'Aaaaarrrgh!'

An even bigger yawn this time, a real jaw-breaker.

Jason broke off. 'Look, am I boring you or something?'

'Say yes!' hissed a voice in Jonathan's ear.

'No, not a bit,' said Jonathan hastily. 'Carry on!'

Jason glared angrily across the table. 'Because if I am, just say so. I wouldn't want to get on the wrong side of you – I gather it's not healthy.'

'What are you on about?'

Jason's easy, pleasant manner had disappeared now, and he was white-faced with rage. 'They tell me things happen to people who try to upset you. Well, you'd better not try any of your little tricks on me!' Suddenly furious, Jason slammed his fist down on the table – right into his pudding bowl which had somehow slid underneath it. A little spray of apples and custard splattered up into his face. Everyone roared with laughter. Everyone but Jason who roared with rage. Jumping to his feet, he hurled himself across the table at Jonathan.

Somehow his feet slid from under him,

and his face came down on the table – right in the bowl of apples and custard which had slid yet again into exactly the right spot.

Jason straightened up, wiping custard out of his eyes.

'Look, I'm sorry,' said Jonathan.

Jason ignored him. White-faced, and dripping with apple pie and custard, he stood up and stalked out of the dining hall.

Timmy gave Jonathan a reproachful look. 'That wasn't very clever, picking on someone on his very first day.'

'What did I do?' protested Jonathan. 'It was just an accident.' From the look on the faces around the table, it was quite clear that no-one believed him.

CHAPTER TWO

Old Friend, New Friend

'Look, Dave, just pack it in, all right?' said Jonathan fiercely to the empty air. He was walking alone, on the way back from the dining hall after lunch.

Dave materialised strolling beside him. 'Me?'

'I've told you, if you must come to school with me, don't muck around.'

'All I did was yawn,' protested Dave. 'I was getting a bit tired of that bloke Jason's round the world in eighty days act.'

'What about the apples and custard attack?'

'He did that himself, most of it anyway. I

just helped a bit.'

'Well, you've got everyone down on me now.'

'What, over that toffee-nosed twit?' said Dave. 'He's the sort of bloke who has to be the big I-am all the time.' He kicked sulkily at a pebble and muttered, 'Can't stand people like that.'

'Come off it, Dave. Maybe he did go on a bit but he was probably just nervous.'

'Take my tip and keep well away from him,' said Dave. 'He's not to be trusted – he's got a funny aura!'

'Funny what?'

'Aura – sort of glowing light you lot have all around you. It's an energy-field or something.'

Jonathan looked hard at Dave. Presumably 'You lot' referred to the living. 'Don't ghosts have them?'

''Course not. We can see 'em though. Some living people can see them as well. You can tell a lot about a bloke from his aura.'

'What's wrong with Jason's then?'

'It's frayed and fuzzy and the colours are

all harsh. Means he's all jangled-up inside.'

'He doesn't look jangled. Seems cool as a cucumber.'

'That's just the outside. It's what's inside that counts.'

'Well, maybe his inside would feel better if his outside wasn't covered with custard! Just leave him alone in future, will you?'

Jonathan drew a deep breath. 'As a matter of fact, I'd be glad if you'd leave everyone alone, teachers, kids, *everyone,* all right?'

'Hang on,' protested Dave. 'It was only a bit of fun.'

'Maybe it was - but your bits of fun make life very awkward for me! Jason thinks I'm some kind of weirdo already, and he's only been here five minutes! No more little tricks, all right?'

'My little tricks have come pretty useful in the past,' said Dave. 'But if that's how you want it . . .'

He vanished in a ghostly huff.

Jonathan sighed. In a way what Dave had said was true enough. He'd helped Jonathan quite a bit, especially in sorting out Basher Briggs, the school bully. But the trouble with Dave's help was that it created as many problems as it solved.

Jason was all neat and clean when he turned up in class after the dinner-break, no trace of custard anywhere.

Jonathan went over to him. 'Look, I'm sorry about that business at lunchtime.'

'Think nothing of it,' said Jason cheerfully. 'Accidents will happen. Sorry I blew up like that.'

They sat at the same work table in the next couple of lessons, and found themselves getting on really well.

Jonathan could still remember what it felt like being a late-arriving new boy, and gave Jason as many useful tips as he could. Like which teachers insisted on work being in strictly on time; which would put up with a bit of lateness; which had filthy tempers; which were pretty easy-going; which had hobbies that could be used to distract them . . . 'Get old Potter started on steam trains and you can forget about geography for the rest of the lesson.'

At the end of the day Jason said suddenly, 'Want to come round tonight?'

'All right, if you like.'

Jason gave him the address and they fixed things up.

In the playground Jonathan bumped into Timmy who asked, 'Coming round tonight?'

'Sorry, I can't. Tomorrow, maybe?'

'Yes, fine, any time,' said Timmy, and wandered away.

Suddenly Jonathan realised he hadn't spoken to Timmy all afternoon.

Dave popped up again when Jonathan was on his way home. He was still in a sulky mood. 'You won't listen, will you? I told you to keep away from that Jason.'

'What do you mean? He's all right when you get to know him.'

'You'll have trouble with him, you'll see.'

'Look, I'll handle things, all right?' said Jonathan.

'If you can,' said Dave. 'Still, suit yourself!'

And with that he disappeared again.

'Good riddance too' thought Jonathan. 'What right's he got to tell me who I can be friends with?'

The visit to Jason's was quite an experience. His mother had rented a big posh house in one of the poshest streets around, the sort of area where the driveways are littered with Bentleys and

Rolls Royces.

Jason seemed to have the house to himself, apart from a quiet smiling man and woman Jason referred to casually as 'our couple.'

'Mum's out at some charity committee meeting,' explained Jason. 'She's usually pretty busy. Come and see my room.'

Like his house, Jason's room was quite something!

It was a big, luxuriously-furnished bed sitting room, and it had just about everything you could want in it. There was a TV set, a hi-fi stereo and a compact disc player as well. The home computer was state-of-the-art high technology, and it had all the latest video games to go with it.

Not that Jason was showing off about all this stuff – he seemed to take it pretty much for granted.

(As Jonathan learned later, he had a wardrobe full of Italian-designed track-suits and flashy American running-shoes. He also had a shockproof, waterproof, everything-proof watch that told the time all round the world, and a mountain bike with about ninety-nine gears.)

They talked for a while, then settled down to play one of the video games. It was called Galactic Rescue and you had to pick up a group of stranded astronauts in your flying saucer, fighting off complicated attacks from a variety of alien nasties at the same time.

(You had five 'lives' and then you were out.)

Jason played brilliantly, rescuing his astronauts in record time, without losing a single life.

When it was his turn, Jonathan got zapped all five times, without getting

anywhere near his astronauts.

Jason did his best not to look too pleased. 'Fancy another game?'

'If you like. I'm rubbish at this, though. You'll only slaughter me again.'

But the second game was very different. This time it was Jason who got zapped. All his shots seemed to miss and he used up all his lives in record time.

Jonathan on the other hand couldn't do anything wrong. All the blasts from the nasties' laser-guns missed by a mile, while he himself zapped an alien with every shot.

As he picked up his last astronaut, Jonathan saw a new figure on the screen. It was a miniature electronic Dave, jumping up and down and waving excitedly. No wonder he'd won so easily – there was a ghost in the computer!

Jason jumped up from the keyboard scowling. 'Well, you certainly picked that up quick enough!'

'I was just lucky,' said Jonathan hurriedly. 'Must be some kind of a bug in your game programe!'

Jason gave Jonathan one of those baffled

looks he was coming to dread. It was the way Huw Hughes had looked at him earlier, and Timmy and lots of others. And it was all Dave's fault!

To Jonathan's relief, Jason's mood suddenly changed. 'Oh well, never mind. It's only a game. Fancy a snack? Coke and burgers all right?'

'Well, if it's no trouble . . . Want me to help you cook?'

Jonathan was quite used to cooking for himself at home, but Jason seemed shocked. 'No, no, they'll do it. I'll just go and tell them.' 'They' presumably being 'the couple' thought Jonathan.

When Jason had gone, Jonathan glared at the computer. 'Come on, Dave, I know you're in there!'

Dave's face appeared on the computer screen, grinning cheekily. 'Wotcha, mate! Enjoy the game?'

'No, I didn't,' said Jonathan grimly. 'I'm telling you! Pack it in!'

Dave looked hurt. 'He was slaughtering you, wasn't he? Don't you want to win?'

'Not if it's you and not me. It's cheating, makes the whole thing pointless.'

'It was only a bit of fun . . .'

'That's where you're wrong, Dave,' said Jonathan furiously. 'I *was* having fun – till you turned up and ruined it! Why don't you just clear off?'

Dave stared back at him, shocked. Then

206

he went – but he didn't go quietly.

As his face vanished from the screen a miniature whirlwind swept round the room, billowing out the curtains and sending books and papers and cushions flying through the air.

As Jason came back into the room, the rushing wind buffeted him aside and swept off down the passage, making rugs billow up and down like waves on a stormy sea. The front door flew open wide then slammed shut with a thunderous crash.

Jason took it all amazingly calmly, almost as if he was used to such goings-on. 'What was *that* all about?'

'Search me,' babbled Jonathan. 'Freak atmospherics, maybe. A gust of wind must have got in through the window and got trapped.'

'Well, whatever it was, I'm glad it's gone!'

'Yes,' said Jonathan. 'So am I . . .'

The female half of the couple came in with a tray of coke, chips and hamburgers, looking astonished at all the mess. She helped them clear it up – there was no real damage, luckily – and disappeared.

The rest of the evening passed off without any more mysterious incidents, much to Jonathan's relief. It looked as if Dave had finally taken the hint.

They finished their snack and chatted – or rather, Jason chatted and Jonathan listened.

At last Jonathan said he had to go.

'Come on, it's early yet,' said Jason.

Jonathan looked at his watch. 'Not for me. Mum and Dad'll freak out – they don't like me out too late on school nights.'

Jason looked surprised. 'My lot couldn't care less what I do, as long as I don't bother them.'

As Jason opened the front door they saw an expensive-looking lady getting out of an expensive-looking car.

She gave Jason a kiss. 'How was the new school, dear?'

'Fine. This is Jonathan, he's in my class.'

'That's nice,' said Jason's mother absently. 'Now, I really must make a few phone calls before it gets too late . . .' She swept into the house.

'That was my mum,' said Jason.

'She seems very nice,' said Jonathan, feeling he ought to say something.

'She's okay, I suppose. Don't see her much, she's usually on her way in, on her way out, or on the telephone!'

Jonathan set off home, turning to wave to Jason at the end of the drive.

Standing alone at the top of the steps, Jason waved back and went inside the big house.

Jonathan expected Dave to appear on the way home, but for once there was no sign of him.

Stranger still, he didn't appear later on. Bedtime was usually Dave's favourite time. He'd materialise sitting cross-legged on the end of the bed and they'd talk over the events of the day. Dave usually seemed quite prepared to talk all night – maybe ghosts didn't need sleep – and usually Jonathan drifted off to sleep with Dave chatting away . . .

Tonight there was no sign of him.

'He's probably just having a bit of a sulk,' thought Jonathan. 'I suppose I was a bit hard on him. He'll be back when he gets over it.'

All the same, thought Jonathan, as he drifted off to sleep, it felt funny without Dave around.

CHAPTER THREE
A Bad Day for Briggsy

There was still no sign of Dave next morning, when Jonathan went to school. He usually popped up for a chat somewhere along the way – but not this time.

Jonathan was still worrying about it as he crossed the playground. 'Wonder if I was too rough on him,' he thought – but he forgot all about Dave as soon as he went into the classroom. Jason was telling a fascinated audience one of his travellers tales - but he broke off as soon as he saw Jonathan. 'There you are, me old mate! Come and sit over here with me. I was just telling the lads about the time I went to

Disneyland. They've got this ride there called Space Mountain. Well, talk about terrifying . . .'

It was as if Jonathan was the one person Jason had really been waiting to see.

Jason broke off again as old Foxy, Mr Fox their form master, came into the room.

'Tell you the rest at break,' he whispered.

Before very long, it seemed as if Jason had always been there. He and Jonathan seemed to spend most of their school days together. They walked home together at the end of the day, and often visited each other's house.

(Jason charmed Jonathan's mum with his friendly smile and his wonderful manners.)

Come to that, Jason seemed to be popular with everyone. The others liked him because he was lively and friendly, full of stories about his colourful life.

'He's a natural athlete,' said Hadley the Games Captain, 'Knows a lot about soccer too. He was telling me about the Continental long game . . .'

Even the teachers liked him. 'The boy's a

pleasure to have in the class,' said Mr Fox
in the staff room. 'Neat, polite, and bright
and intelligent as well.'

'He appreciates art, too,' said Huw
Hughes. 'The art galleries and museums
he's visited . . .'

No doubt about it, Jason was a
Superstar.

Jonathan couldn't help feeling proud of being picked out to be his best friend.

Of course, it meant he didn't see too much of Timmy any more. Somehow Jason and Timmy just didn't seem to get on.

The only shadow over things was the continued absence of Dave. He hadn't reappeared at all since that first night at Jason's house. In a way, of course, it was a relief not to have him popping up and causing trouble. 'After all,' thought Jonathan, 'that's what I wanted all along.'

But he missed Dave all the same.

Still, he had Jason for a friend now. Not that things were all sweetness and light about Jason either. Jason had funny moods.

Most of the time he was bright and cheerful and full of beans. But occasionally, just occasionally, he'd turn up in a bleak and savage mood, lashing out at anyone who irritated him. Jason seemed almost ill at times like these, white-faced and tense.

Once when Jonathan asked him about it, he just muttered, 'Look, I get these headaches, migraines, they're called. Just leave me alone, can't you? I'll be all right.'

Usually on these occasions he disappeared for a bit, then turned up later, brighter than ever.

Looking back afterwards, Jonathan decided that the real trouble started on the day that Basher Briggs had his accident.

It was in the playground just after school, and Briggs was moaning about his lost fiver. According to him, he'd brought it to school that morning and it had disappeared during the course of the day. They had all searched the classroom and the cloakroom and the playground without success.

Recently there had been quite a few cases of mysteriously missing money. One theory was that some kind of sneak thief was getting into the school, wandering round unnoticed in the crowd, and lifting whatever he could find.

Although everyone had rallied round in the hunt for the missing fiver Briggsy wasn't satisfied. He was still giving everyone a hard time at the end of school.

'Somebody must have it,' he insisted. 'I

bet I dropped it and one of you lot picked it up and kept it. If I find out who it is . . .'

'Oh do leave off, Briggsy,' said Jason wearily. 'Nobody stole it, you just lost it. And after all, it was only a fiver . . .'

'Oh, *only* a fiver,' sneered Briggs, mimicking Jason's voice. 'A fiver's nothing to you, is it Jason? Well, we're not all rolling in it!'

Jason winced at the loud, grating voice. 'Please, Briggsy, just shut up and go away!'

'Don't you tell me to shut up!' Briggs took a step towards Jason, clenching meaty fists.

Jonathan stepped hurriedly between them. 'Just leave it, Briggsy. It's rotten luck about the fiver, but there's no point in taking it out on Jason, or on anyone else.'

'I'll sort you out as well, Jonno!' threatened Briggs.

'No you won't,' said Jonathan. 'You tried before, remember?'

Briggs hesitated. He'd tried getting tough when Jonathan had first come to the school. Thanks to the unseen Dave, he'd suffered a humiliating defeat.

Briggs glared angrily at him, and Jonathan tried to look tough and confident. It was all bluff, of course, with Dave no longer around, but luckily Briggsy didn't know that.

He turned away, and stumped over to the bike sheds. Unchaining his bike, he got on and pedalled away.

Jason rubbed his forehead. 'Stupid great

oaf . . .' He was sitting on the school steps, looking really ill.

'Oh, just ignore him,' said Jonathan. 'Look, are you all right?'

Before Jason could reply, there came a distant yell of alarm. Jonathan turned, and saw Briggs pedalling frantically down the cycle path, yelling aloud at the same time. 'Help! Help, stop me!' The cycle path led directly on to the main road, and there were all sorts of notices warning you to ride slowly and emerge onto the road with care.

Briggsy was ignoring them, pedalling at top speed towards the stream of traffic.

'Briggsy, pack it in,' yelled Jonathan. 'You'll get yourself killed!'

He started running after him, though there was no hope of getting there in time.

Still yelling, Briggsy shot straight towards the busy road. At the last possible moment, he swerved aside, and rode straight into a tree at the edge of the pavement.

Jonathan pounded breathlessly up to him. Briggsy was all tangled up with his bike at the foot of the tree, blood running from a cut on his chin.

Jonathan helped him to disentangle himself and get to his feet. 'You all right?'

'Yeah, I think so.'

'What do you think you were playing at?'

'Wasn't me,' said Briggs dazedly. 'It was the bike. It suddenly started going faster. Then the brakes wouldn't work . . . I turned into that tree on purpose to stop myself.'

Jonathan picked up the bike. The handlebars had been wrenched round and the front wheel was buckled. He spun the back wheel and squeezed the brakes. The brake block clamped down on the wheel, stopping it dead. Jonathan tried the front brake. That seemed to be working perfectly too.

Jason came up to them. 'What happened?'

'Search me. Briggsy's bike seems to have run away with him.'

Jason looked at the battered bike. 'I expect he was just pedalling too hard. He did stomp off in a rage, remember.' He looked at the equally battered Briggs, who was dabbing at the cut on his forehead with a grimy handkerchief. 'Poor old Briggsy, you have had a rotten day.' Jason fished in his pocket. He took out a crumpled piece of blue paper which he handed to Briggs.

'Here, why don't you take this?'

Briggsy stared at it. 'This is a fiver!'

'Plenty more where that came from,' said Jason cheerfully. 'Go on, you take it.'

'Well, thanks,' said Briggs. Staring at the

crumpled fiver as if he couldn't believe it was real, he set off for home, wheeling his wonky bike.

Jonathan looked at Jason. 'You're crazy!'

'I felt so sorry for the poor old twerp.' Jason grinned. 'You couldn't treat me to a can of coke on the way home, could you? My attack of mad generosity has left me skint!'

Jonathan shook his head. 'Sometimes I

can't make you out, Jason. Either you're rolling in it or you're completely broke – sometimes both in the same day! And as for giving away fivers . . .'

'Well, easy come, easy go,' said Jason. 'Come on, let's get out of this dump.' He hesitated. 'It seems to be true what they say!'

'What's that?'

'Well, that funny things happen to people who upset you. I mean, old Briggsy threatens to thump you, and next thing he and his bike are wrapped round a tree.'

'Don't talk rubbish,' said Jonathan uneasily. 'It was just an accident like you said. Briggsy was pedalling too hard and lost control.'

But as they walked along, he couldn't help wondering if Jason was right.

Maybe Dave was back after all . . .

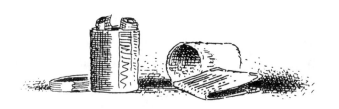

CHAPTER FOUR

The Accident

Things went from bad to worse after that.

For one thing the stealing went on – it not only went on, it increased.

The contents of a tin full of dinner money disappeared from one of the classrooms. A teacher's wallet vanished from his coat in the staff room. Petty cash was taken from a locked drawer in the canteen.

It was at this point that the Head called in the police. A large, grim-looking constable appeared in school, accompanied by a thin, sharp-faced young man from the local CID.

They questioned the whole school, first in

whole classes then separately, though always with a teacher or a parent present. When his turn came, Jonathan just said he hadn't taken any money and didn't know who had. Even though he hadn't done anything, he found being questioned a pretty scary experience.

'It's funny how you feel guilty just for being there,' he said afterwards.

Timmy nodded. 'I'd have confessed to the Great Train Robbery if they'd asked.'

'They didn't scare me,' boasted Briggsy.

'No?' said Jonathan. 'Well you were pale

and quiet when you came out – which is quite a change for you.'

Briggsy, now his usual red-faced and noisy self again, glared at him, started to speak and then shut up again.

'Well, I enjoyed my little interrogation,' said Jason. 'That CID man was very bright. We had a chat about Continental police methods. I reckon all this mass questioning's a waste of time. The innocent ones can't tell them anything, and the guilty one won't!'

For a while it looked as if Jason was right. But a day or so later, the school was full of rumours that the police had found their man – or rather boy.

It was a kid called Ricky in another class. Crop-headed and tough-looking, he had what the police called a 'disturbed family background' and apparently he'd been in trouble before over nicking things from the local shops.

'Sounds a bit too easy to me,' said Jonathan when he heard. 'I mean, just because the poor kid's already been in trouble . . .'

'It's not just that,' said Timmy. 'Apparently Ricky's always broke – but just recently he's been chucking money about. He *said* he won it on a bet.'

But, as it turned out, Ricky really had won money betting. A local bookmaker remembered him putting a pound on a twenty to one outsider that actually won.

And just to clinch things, money was stolen from the school secretary's handbag on the very day Ricky was at the police station being questioned, and Ricky had to be released with apologies.

That was the day the trouble really started.

The Head kept everyone back after school for a special meeting. He told everyone what had happened and went on, 'I'm very glad to say that Ricky's been completely cleared, and I want to apologise to him on behalf of the school. Some of us, myself included, were a bit too quick to jump to conclusions.'

Ricky sniffed and tried to look noble and persecuted.

The Head went on, 'Pleased as we all are

for Ricky, we musn't forget that the thief, the real thief is still undetected. I want to say two things. First, it is up to us, all of us, to give the thief no more opportunities. Bring money to school only when absolutely necessary, and take good care of it at all times.'

He looked sternly around the silent hall. 'Secondly, I want to ask whoever is responsible to stop this disastrous course of behaviour at once, and to come privately to see me. Stealing isn't clever, it's merely stupid, and sooner or later the thief is bound to be caught . . .'

As they all went out of the hall and into the playground, Jason had one of his headaches and was in a lousy mood. 'Fancy keeping us all back just to hear that. Why couldn't it have waited till tomorrow's assembly?'

Jonathan was feeling pretty fed up too. The unpleasantness over the stealing seemed to have been dragging on forever, and now it still wasn't over.

'The whole thing's a right pain if you ask me. And you're right, there was no need to

keep us all in like that . . . Flaming fascist!'
Jonathan broke off hurriedly as a tall, still-
youngish man with rumpled tweed jacket
and untidy hair appeared at the top of the
steps. Usually the Head would give you a
smile and a wave, or even stop for a chat,
but this time he marched straight past,
grim-faced.

'Charming!' muttered Jason. 'You'd think
he suspected *us*!'

Jonathan shrugged. 'Probably suspects
everyone. Come on . . .'

They started to follow the Head across
the playground. Suddenly they heard a
faint grating, slithering sound, from
somewhere high up behind them. A dark
shape flashed downwards through the air,

struck the Head a glancing blow and then shattered on the ground. The Head was on the ground too, blood pouring from his forehead.

At this point Jason became the hero of the hour. All grumbles forgotten, he raced across the playground and knelt beside the fallen man. Producing a clean white handkerchief – trust Jason to have one, thought Jonathan – he folded it into a pad and staunched the bleeding. 'Doesn't look too deep . . .' He looked up at Jonathan. 'I'll stay with him, you go and call an ambulance . . .'

'No, no,' said the Head faintly. 'I'm all right . . .' He managed to sit up.

Jason gave him the folded handkerchief to hold against the cut. 'Are you sure, sir? Did you lose consciousness at all, even for a minute because if you did . . .'

'No, I wasn't knocked out. More startled than hurt, I think . . . What hit me?'

Jonathan looked at the black shiny fragments at their feet and picked one up. 'It's slate, sir. A whole slate must have come off the roof . . .'

'Just one slate, off a newly-repaired roof – and I have to be standing underneath!'

'One of those freak accidents,' said Jason. 'It must have just clipped you in passing – could have been a lot worse.'

'A freak accident,' said the Head. He looked at Jonathan for a moment, then turned back to Jason. 'There's a first-aid box in my office . . .'

'Leave it to me, sir' said Jason cheerfully. He helped the Head to his feet and supported him as he went shakily up the steps and across the foyer and into his office. Not quite sure what to do, Jonathan trailed behind them.

Timothy came running up. 'What happened? What's going on?'

'The Head had a bit of an accident. He's okay, Jason's looking after him. Tell everyone not to fuss.'

Jonathan followed the others into the office and closed the door. Jason was just settling the Head in a chair. 'Where's the first-aid box, sir?'

'Bottom right hand drawer of my desk. . . It's locked . . . The Head fished out a bunch of keys. 'It's this one. . .'

'I'll get it,' said Jonathan, keen to help. The Head gave him the key and he opened the deep double drawer.

'There's just a sort of blue bag, sir . . .'

Jonathan lifted the blue bag, which seemed to rustle and clink at the same time.

'No leave that alone,' snapped the Head. 'There's a white box with a red cross on it, under the bag at the back of the drawer.'

Jonathan took out the box, replaced the bag, and carried the box over to Jason. In no time at all, the Head's cut was covered with a neat pad of gauze held in place with sticking plaster.

The Head looked at himself in the mirror. 'A very neat job, Jason.'

'Dad made me take a first-aid course, sir, when we were doing so much travelling. It's often come in handy!'

The Head put back the first-aid box and then locked the drawer. 'Well, thank you both for your help. I assure you I'll be all right now.'

'Call a doctor if you start feeling faint or giddy, sir,' said Jason. 'In fact it might be a good idea to see one anyway. I don't think that cut needs stitches, but you never know.'

Jonathan was silent and preoccupied as he came out of school and set off home.

'You all right?' asked Jason at the corner where they separated.

'I'm not feeling too wonderful,' admitted Jonathan.

'Delayed shock,' said Jason. 'You go home

and have a cuppa and a nice quiet evening in. See you tomorrow.'

Whistling cheerfully, Jason marched away.

It wasn't the shock of the Head's accident that was worrying Jonathan. It was the look the Head had given him afterwards. 'Does he really think I caused the accident?' he thought. 'Come to that, did I cause it? First Briggsy, now this!'

Jonathan's secret fear was that Dave was behind both accidents. Was it some misguided attempt to help him? Or, worse still, was Dave deliberately trying to get him into trouble?

As he turned into his street Jonathan whispered, 'Dave, where are you? Come out and tell me what's going on!'

But apart from the rustling of the leaves in the wind, there was no reply.

CHAPTER FIVE

Robbery!

Jason was the centre of attention by the time Jonathan got into school. Everyone was crowding round asking about his heroic rescue of the Head.

'All I did was stick a bit of plaster on,' he protested. 'It could just as well have been old Jonno here.'

'Maybe he'd already done his bit,' said Briggsy.

Jason stared at him. 'You what?'

'Well, we all know funny things happen when Jonno's around.'

'Don't be such an idiot,' yelled Jonathan angrily.

Briggs paled and backed away. 'All right, only joking . . .'

'I'd watch your step at break-time, Briggsy,' someone shouted. 'You might finish up with a plaster on your bonce as well!'

It wasn't the best start to the day.

But the end was worse – far worse.

At the end of the very last lesson – maths with Foxy as it happened – a messenger from the Head appeared. Jason and Jonathan were to report to the Headmaster's office.

'I expect he wants his plaster changed, Jason,' someone shouted.

Timmy said, 'I expect he's going to give you both a medal!'

It was clear from the expression on the Head's face that no medals were going to be handed out.

'I should like you to cast your minds back to last night,' he said abruptly. 'After my accident we came in here. I gave one of you the key to open the drawer to get the first-aid box – you, wasn't it Jonathan?'

'Yes, sir.'

'And to get at the box you had to move a large blue bag. Do you have any idea what was in it?'

'Money I suppose, sir. It was a blue bag, the kind banks use, and it rustled and clinked.'

The Head nodded. 'The bag held the last instalment of the money for the school ski trip – almost a thousand pounds, most of it

in cheques, but a certain amount in notes and coins. One boy had forgotten his instalment. I was waiting for him to bring it today so I could bank the whole sum at once. The instalment arrived, I went to put it with the rest, but the bag had disappeared.' He paused. 'It was quite exceptional for that bag to be in the drawer overnight. And, as far as I am aware, you two are the only ones, besides myself, who knew it was there.'

There was a nasty silence.

Then Jonathan said. 'I saw the bag last night, sir – for the first and only time. The last I saw of it was when you locked it in the drawer again.'

The Head nodded. 'Jason?'

'I didn't even notice the thing.' Jason paused. 'Look, I don't quite know how to say this sir, but I don't actually need to steal. My father gives me a good allowance, and if I want anything extra, I just have to ask for it.'

The Head nodded without comment. He looked from one to the other. 'This can't go on you know,' he said. 'We're a big, modern school with hundreds of pupils. Boys bring in money, the school uses valuable equipment . . . The Science Lab alone has just taken delivery of new computer equipment worth thousands of pounds. It can't all be guarded all the time, not unless we turn the place into a prison . . . The person responsible for these thefts must be found and stopped.'

When no-one spoke the Head went on, 'Would either of you object to opening your school lockers for me?'

'No sir,' said Jason and Jonathan both together.

They went back through the now deserted school, their footsteps echoing

hollowly, to the lockers in the corridor outside their classroom.

They'd managed to get lockers side by side. Jason opened his first. It was amazingly neat and tidy, everything folded and in its place, books, papers, football boot, PE kit . . .

The Head studied it and nodded. 'Jonathan?'

Jonathan opened his locker and three books and a pair of trainers fell out. Inside the locker, not neatly arranged but shoved in anyhow was much the same stuff as in Jason's.

The Head peered into the clutter. 'What's that wadded up in the far corner?'

'PE kit I think, sir.'

Jonathan pulled out the blue bundle. It wasn't a pair of PE shorts at all. It was a blue bag, the kind the banks use to keep money in.

The Head took it from him. 'Well?'

'I didn't take the money,' said Jonathan. 'Someone put that bag there.'

'When? Was it here when you opened your locker this morning?'

'I just don't know. It could have been, I
didn't notice. You can see the state my
locker's in.'

Jason said, 'Jonathan, why didn't you tell
me? I could have helped . . .'

'Jason, you can go,' said the Head. 'I'd be

grateful if you'd keep quiet about this.'

'Not a word, sir,' promised Jason. 'Jonathan, if there's anything I can do, anything at all . . .'

He gave Jonathan another worried look and hurried away.

The Head gestured to Jonathan to close his locker. Then, carrying the blue bag, he led the way back to his office.

Sitting down at his desk, he tipped out the contents of the bag – a pile of pink and blue paper oblongs.

'Cheques still here, as you might expect,' he muttered. 'There was only about twenty-five pounds in cash. The thief must have been disappointed.'

'Look, sir, I know it looks bad. I came in your office when you were hurt, I picked up the bag when I got the first-aid box, then I put it back, and that was the last time I saw it until now. I knew it was there, but I didn't steal it.'

The Head watched him gravely, but made no reply.

Jonathan struggled to think of something else to say. 'My family's not rich like Jason's but I don't need to steal either. Look sir, I know it wasn't me and I can't believe it was Jason. Isn't it at least possible that someone else knew about the money?'

'I can't see how, I'm afraid.' The Head paused. 'There's something else, Jonathan. These accidents, the one with Briggs and his bike, and my little affair . . .' He touched the plaster on his forehead. 'Now, I've come to accept that odd things happen around you, but this sort of thing's way over the top. Briggs could easily have been killed.' He touched the plaster on his forehead. 'Come to that, so could I.'

'Listen, sir,' said Jonathan desperately. 'If you think back about everything that's happened since I came to this school, has there ever once been anything really dangerous? Has anyone ever been badly hurt, has there ever been any serious damage?'

'So you had nothing to do with sending Briggs on a kamikaze run into the traffic, or crowning me with a roof-slate?'

'Nothing at all, sir.'

The Head looked thoughtfully at him.

'It's true that up to now your pranks have been harmless. But these accidents were ugly and dangerous - like the stealing. The question is, could the same person be responsible for the accidents and the thefts

– and is that person you?'

'That's two questions, sir. The answers are yes – though I don't see how – and no, in that order. Not unless I'm a Jekyll and Hyde and don't know I'm doing it. What happens now?'

'To be honest, I've no idea. I'm reluctant to believe you're the thief but . . .' He nodded towards the blue bag. 'Do you keep that locker locked, by the way?'

'Yes, but those padlocks are dead easy to pick. We all do it to play jokes, or when we've lost our keys.'

'All right, off you go. We'll talk again when we've both had a chance to think things over. Don't say anything about all this meanwhile, and come to school as usual in the morning.'

Leaving the Head brooding at his desk, Jonathan went out of the school and made his way home.

Luckily his parents had gone out to visit a neighbour so they weren't there to notice his preoccupied state.

Jonathan ate a solitary supper of

burgers, beans and chips and went up to his room. Stretched out on his bed, he lay staring into space. How was he going to get through school tomorrow . . .

Suddenly a kid in shorts and shirt and grimy tennis shoes was sitting cross-legged on the end of the bed and grinning cheekily at him.

'Well, you're right in it now, mate, aren't you?' said the ghostly apparition cheerfully. 'Maybe next time, you'll listen to your Uncle Dave!'

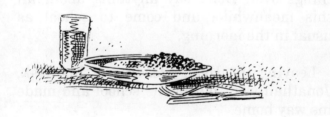

CHAPTER SIX

Showdown

Jonathan's first reaction was sheer relief. 'Dave! There you are at last.'

Now Dave was back, everything was going to be all right. His next reaction was sheer indignation. 'Where've you been?'

'What do you mean, where've I been? Told me to push off, didn't you?'

'All right, so I got a bit ratty with you. I didn't mean you to disappear forever.'

'Well, I haven't, have I?' said Dave. 'Don't worry, mate, I didn't go just because you yelled at me. I've been checking things out on the astral plane – that and building my strength up. We're up against something

247

really dangerous this time.'

'The real thief, you mean?'

'Stealing's the least of it. I'm talking about psychic attacks, mate.'

'You mean the accidents? Briggsy's bike and the roof-slate that clobbered the Head?'

'That's right – only they weren't accidents.'

'Come on, Dave, out with it. What's been going on, and who's behind it?'

'You wouldn't believe me if I told you!'

'So what do we do now?'

'We go round and see your mate Jason.'

'Does he know who caused those accidents?'

'No, he doesn't know anything about it. But he can put us in touch all the same,' said Dave – and refused to say any more.

Jonathan left his parents a note that he was going round to Jason's house, and might be a bit late, and they set off.

It was raining by now and the wind was getting up. It was almost the proverbial dark and stormy night, thought Jonathan. Normally he might have felt a bit scared going through the dimly lit streets, but with Dave beside him, everything seemed all right. No need to worry about ghosts with a ghost for a friend. Then he remembered Dave's words. 'This something dangerous we're after – is it a ghost?'

Dave shook his head. 'It isn't the ghost of anybody dead, if that's what you mean. You might say it was the ghost of someone still alive . . .'

By now they'd reached Jason's house and Dave came to a sudden halt. 'Look!' he whispered, and pointed.

A tall figure was slipping out of the front gate.

Jonathan opened his mouth to yell, but Dave clamped a grimy hand over it.

'Don't yell – follow!'

Jason was wearing black jeans, black trainers, a black polo neck and a black anorak with a hood. The shoulder-bag he was carrying was black as well, and he was almost invisible in the shadows. But they managed to stay on his trail, keeping as far behind as they could without losing him.

Soon Jonathan realised he was following a familiar route. Jason was heading for school.

He realised something else as well. The storm actually seemed to be *following* Jason, the wind springing up as the tall, black-clad figure strode by, following behind him in a kind of wake. Jonathan was just about to point this out, when Dave suddenly turned and leaped at him, shoving him back. A huge elm branch

crashed to the ground, just where Jonathan had been standing.

'Watch out, and stick by me,' whispered Dave. 'This isn't your ordinary storm. This one's dangerous!'

Jason led them round to the side of the school. A black van was parked there, waiting. He had a quick word with the driver and then moved round to the low wall at the back.

Dave and Jonathan followed, and saw Jason swing himself over the wall.

Jonathan scrambled over the wall after him, to find Dave materialising on the other side.

'Quick, this way,' whispered Dave, and led him across the darkened playground.

They found Jason crouching by a ground-floor window, busy with clippers and what looked like a length of wire. He slid open the window and slipped through, leaving it open behind him. A few moments later, Dave and Jonathan followed after him.

Jonathan paused to examine the wire that ran along the top of the window. It had been cut and then the two ends re-joined with clips to the ends of a long piece of wire which bridged the gap between them. Jason had short-circuited the alarm system.

Sickened, Jonathan realised that Jason was showing all the skills of a professional thief.

Jonathan slipped through the window and he and Dave followed Jason along the dark corridors of the darkened school. His trainers were silent on the stone floors and he felt rather like a ghost himself as they crept silently through the shadows. They saw Jason crouching by the locked door of the Science Lab. There was a click and the door sprang open.

Jason went inside, and Jonathan and Dave crept to the door and peered inside.

The familiar surroundings of the lab looked strangely sinister in the darkness, and it would have been no surprise to see the giant lumpy shape of Frankenstein's monster stretched out on a slab, with the good Doctor himself crouching over it.

Jason moved across to the electronic section in the far corner of the lab. He looked round the array of keyboards and dials and monitors.

Before Dave could stop him, Jonathan stepped into the room. 'Hard to know where to start, isn't it?'

Jason stared unbelievingly at him. 'How did you get here?'

'I followed you.'

'You know then?'

'I do now.'

'Look, Jonathan, I can explain,' said Jason hurriedly.

'Go on then.'

'These people, crooks, I owe them lots of money, never mind what for.' Jason was talking so fast that he was almost babbling. 'I thought I'd got away from them but they traced me here. They threatened me, said I had to pay them back something every week, but it kept going up and I gave them

all I could but it was never enough. I thought the ski-holiday money would be enough to settle with them but it was nearly all cheques so it was useless.'

'Why did you have to plant that bag on me?'

Jason looked surprised. 'Well, obviously the Head was going to suspect one of us. It was you or me!'

'And what are you doing here?'

'I told them what the Head said, about thousands of pounds worth of electronic equipment . . . They agreed to take equipment instead of money if it was good enough but I'm not sure what to take . . .'

He looked at Jonathan as if he actually expected him to decide. 'You could help me Jonathan, we could share . . .'

'Look, Jason, pack it in, it's over,' said Jonathan wearily. 'I advise you to go to the police - and I warn you, first thing in the morning I'm going to the Head. After all, it's you or me.'

Jason's face twisted with anger. 'No! You mustn't do that!' He glared at Jonathan and raised his hand threateningly.

Suddenly an eerie glow appeared around his body . . .

A heavy glass jar whizzed across the room and smashed against the wall by Jonathan's head.

A lamp beside him blazed into light and exploded, showering him with broken glass.

'Look out!' yelled a voice beside him. It was Dave. He tugged Jonathan back as a heavy wooden cupboard toppled over and crashed onto the spot where he'd been standing. Before Jason could attack again, Dave leapt forward and confronted him, stretching out his hands as if to hold Jason off. There was a glow around Dave as well, and a shaft of light sprang from his outstretched hands. The two bodies glowed and crackled with energy.

To his horror, Jonathan saw that Dave seemed to be getting the worst of it. Jason was bigger and stronger, packed with the energy that comes from hatred. Jonathan sensed that Dave was too young and too inexperienced to deal with him.

As the two figures stood locked in silent struggle, a storm of psychic energy swirled about them.

With Jason looming menacingly over him, the glow around Dave began to fade. Dave himself began fading away to nothingness. Breaking free of his paralysis, Jonathan leaped forward to stand beside him. 'No, Dave!' he yelled. 'Don't give in –

fight him!' Concentrating furiously, Jonathan fought to add his mental energy to Dave's.

The glow round Dave steadied and became bright again. But the energy glow around Jason was brighter too, and now Jonathan could feel its force, trying to wipe him out. Desperately he struggled to hold on.

Suddenly the glow round Jason flared up in a silent explosion of light. Jason screamed and crumpled to the ground, like a puppet whose strings have been cut, just as the Head and the young CID man rushed into the lab.

Jonathan went to help Jason up.

Jason opened his eyes and looked at him in surprise. 'Hello, Jonathan. It's over now, isn't it?'

'Yes, it's all over,' said Jonathan.

Jason rose slowly and slumped wearily onto a lab stool. 'Thank goodness . . .'

He looked at the Head and the CID man. 'Listen, I'm the one who's been doing the stealing, all of it, ever since I arrived here. I took the holiday money and planted the bag in Jonathan's locker. I came here tonight to steal electronic equipment, there are two blokes in a van outside waiting to help me.'

'Not any more there aren't,' said the CID man. 'You come along to the station with me, sonny, and we'll get in touch with your parents and sort it all out.'

Gently but firmly the CID man led him out. Jason paused in the doorway, and gave Jonathan a smile, and in spite of himself Jonathan smiled back.

The CID man led Jason away.

It was the last time Jonathan ever saw him.

He realised the Head was talking to him.

'And just what are you doing here, Jonathan?'

Crossing his fingers behind his back Jonathan said rapidly, 'I was going to call on Jason when I saw him come out of his house so I followed him here and caught him stealing. I tried to stop him and he got a bit violent.'

The Head looked thoughtfully at the broken glass. 'Yes, I can see he did . . . Well, it's not the most convincing story I ever heard, but it will have to do. You'd better get off home. Come and see me first thing tomorrow.'

That night at bedtime Jonathan talked things over with Dave. It was great having his old mate perched on the end of the bed again, and Jonathan realised just how much he'd missed him. Dave seemed pleased to be back, and grateful too. 'I was dead lucky there. If you hadn't joined in I'd have been wiped out.'

'Listen,' said Jonathan, 'there's a whole lot I still don't understand. All right, Jason was stealing because he was desperate for money. But why was he so desperate? And what about all that weird business in the lab – and those mysterious accidents?'

'Well, I can explain that – but it's a bit complicated, even for me. You ever heard about poltergeists?'

'German for noisy ghost,' said Jonathan. 'They chuck a few plates about, smash cups, slam doors . . . Harmless nuisances usually.'

'Right, well to start with a poltergeist isn't a proper ghost at all, not the way I am.'

'What is it then?'

'Sort of random psychic energy – from a living person - an unhappy person.' Dave settled himself more comfortably. 'Every time you get a poltergeist there's a disturbed kid around, usually a teenager, very often a girl. The kid's angry and unhappy and the mental energy spills out and smashes plates or whatever.'

'It does the sort of things the kid doesn't dare do in real life,' said Jonathan impatiently. 'But Jason did more than smash crockery.'

'Yes, but he was a very powerful sort of poltergeist. If the force is very strong, it develops, gets more directional. If anyone annoyed Jason *at certain times*, something nasty was liable to happen to them. Briggsy was annoying Jason as well as you, the Head kept Jason in. The poltergeist's got no sense of proportion, see, it just lashes out.'

'So Jason didn't even know he was doing it?'

Dave yawned. 'That's right. What we don't know is what got poor old Jason so screwed up that his poltergeist started to take over.'

Jonathan learned the answer to that next day in the Head's office.

The Head held out a crumpled paper bag, filled with multi-coloured pills and capsules. 'Drugs!' he said, with loathing in his voice. 'Uppers, downers, ecstasy pills, all kinds of the filthy stuff . . .'

He tossed the bag on the desk. 'Jason went to some posh private school before he came here. He got mixed up in it there – and he got into debt to the drug dealers too. They followed him here and started coming down on him for money - money for more drugs, money they said he owed them. The poor kid got desperate and started stealing.'

'How did you and that policeman turn up like that?'

'I suspected Jason pretty early on.'

'How come, sir?'

'Well, the trouble didn't start until *after* he arrived – and he just felt wrong, off-key somehow. When the holiday money was stolen it had to be him or you – and I just couldn't believe it was you. Finding the bag in your locker was all too pat somehow. So I dropped that hint about valuable equipment in the lab and persuaded that young detective to join me in watching the place.'

'What happens to Jason now?'

'His parents have whipped him off to a private sanatorium. When he's better they're taking him abroad again. We'll just have to hope he'll be all right. They've left money to cover all the thefts, so I don't think anyone will press charges.'

'Watch out for old Briggsy then, sir. Jason pinched a fiver off him but he gave it back. I bet Briggsy still claims!'

Ignoring this, the Head gave Jonathan a stern look. 'Well, all this explains the stealing – but there are other things to be explained. What about all these mysterious accidents?'

'I don't think you need worry about them any more,' said Jonathan. 'Did you ever hear about poltergeists?'

He gave the Head a quick version of Dave's theory.

The Head frowned. 'All sounds pretty far-fetched to me . . .'

To his horror, Jonathan saw that the water jug on the side table behind the Head's desk was rising slowly in the air. Dave was preparing to give him a practical